BROTHERS OF BLOOD

A NEW ORLEANS VAMPYRE NOVELLA

J.T. PATTEN

HEL

To my wife, Shilpa.

"Let's go to New Orleans," she suggested.

Next thing I knew, we'd accepted the discreetly handed business card and secret directions.
As we hurried up St. Ann Street, we looked back at the moon—and the Carter house.
"The vampire sent us," we soon told the man at the gate and passed him the paper.
He unlocked the hidden doorway.

We danced with the green fairy.
Smiled. Kissed. Beamed from the view.
And the rest was history.
Forever.

First edition cover copyright 2023 by J.T. Patten

Cover photography by Braeden Swanson; Cover artistry by SaberCore23-ArtStudio and HELBOUND Productions

HELBOUND Productions first edition eBook

August 2023 ISBN 979-8-9873005-3-4

HELBOUND Productions first edition trade paperback

August 2023 ISBN 979-8-9873005-4-1

A WARNING TO THE READER

This book contains subject material that includes violence, abusive, and/or graphic scenes and descriptions some readers may find disturbing or triggering. In particular, it can be difficult to know what psychological abuse is, especially when it occurs with other forms of abuse and mistreatment. This book exhibits forms of physical and emotional abuse by a vampire compelling or "brainwashing" victims, grooming them for a life with the undead. The author has purposely laid out the chapter titles to highlight stages and elements so readers may recognize mental abuse in their own lives, or that of others.

If you are or have been abused, it is not your fault. You are not alone.

"The vampire is an outsider. He's the perfect metaphor for those things. He's someone who looks human and sounds human, but is not a human, so he's always on the margins."

— *ANNE RICE, AUTHOR,* **INTERVIEW WITH THE VAMPIRE**

PROLOGUE
A LEGEND IS BORN

J ust past her eleventh birthday, Alyson Adnarok woke in an anguished daze, her head throbbing and vision blurry, finding it difficult to open her eyelids. Everything around her seemed dark and obscure, with her other senses slow to return - until Alyson smelled it. The faint stench of death and decay crept up her nostrils. It sent shudders through her, reminding her she was still alive in this nightmare of captivity, as she realized her arms were bound tightly at her sides to a chair, her forearms cut raw by rough ropes that ripped into her young skin.

She tried to scream, but the damp gag in her mouth muffled any sound. As her eyesight slowly returned, she recognized the silhouettes of her captors looming over her. Two disheveled men with twisted features and malicious grins. They wore ragged clothes that reeked of filth and decay, like creatures risen from the depths of hell.

One said, "Welcome back, little Briar Rose," with a morbid laugh. "We thought we would have to wake up our little Sleeping Beauty with a bucket of cold water...but there is no water." He shrugged and laughed again, the disgusting sound hurting her ears.

Memories flickered in her mind, shattered fragments of how

she'd ended up here. It had been around dusk, walking home from the market. They'd grabbed her from the shadows and hit her so hard on the head that she blacked out. Now she was here, in this dark and foul-smelling place, bound and helpless.

One of them loosened the rope, and his tight grip cut her soft skin. He slashed one of her wrists, then the other. She almost fainted at the sight and sound. That would have been a mercy. When her flesh was first slit, the other man stood back, waiting. Anxious. Feral. At the sight of the bloodletting surge, he became manic, lunging wildly for her wrist, only to be shoved aside as the cutter took the first lap.

Undeterred, the cast-off carnivore nudged back to the crimson spillage, nestling in with his partner like two feeding hyenas gorging on their kill. Slurping and lapping away at her fresh, fledgling taste. Growling and gnashing as the other got too close.

The two men continued nursing from the child like wild animals for days, their mouths dripping with her fresh blood. After each feeding, they would redress her wounds, only to cut again hours later.

Surrounding her were others also secured to chairs. Tied tight like tourniquets at the arms and legs. Bound across the mouth. Two who had been sitting in the silent circle when she'd first arrived had been dragged dead into another room when the brothers could feed from their life juice no more. The empty chairs were soon refilled with fresh essence.

For hours, the two men would taunt their prey, threatening other unspeakable horrors.

The trapped meat, like Alyson, could barely keep their eyes open, heads drooping as their organs failed to replenish vital fluids and exhaustion dissipated any urge to fight. To survive.

But even in her weakened state, Alyson never lost hope. She knew she had to escape, or she would never see her family again. She prayed the opportunity may come, studied the cloaked windows for a clue of her whereabouts.

Had it been days or weeks they'd feasted on her very life? She heard them say the word, "brother." Were these monsters a family?

The brothers would come and go. Leaving the flat just before daylight and returning with the nauseating smell of fish and fuel oil just after dark, which added to the hanging odor of body rot.

Through endless nights and nightmares, another morning arrived. By the look of scant light in the room, a faint beam passing through a curtain crack, it was nearly time for their departure.

Alyson struggled against the ropes, but they remained tight, her strength sickly and frail.

One of her captors, who spied her futile efforts from a dark corner without her noticing, cackled. "Don't bother," he spat. "*Everyone* has the same idea. Same attempt. Same end." He drew his finger slowly across his neck, then let his head flop to the side.

The two brothers left as usual, but this time one returned before the silence following their departure could even be enjoyed.

Alyson's panic increased as he ran towards her. His pupils were black and large, his jaw clenched. She had never seen him move so fast.

She braced for a blow.

"Run," he snarled, his fingers fumbling behind her. Once her binds were unknotted, he dashed back for the door. "Free the others if you wish."

Alyson heard his loud footfalls but not the locking click she'd grown accustomed to.

Did he leave it open?

Alyson questioned for a second if it was some cruel joke. A test? Some sick game the brothers played when they got bored. She waited for a while, expecting a demeaning laugh to echo through the halls. But it never came, and the brother's sense of urgency told her time was of the essence. She freed one raw hand from the ropes, then the second before quickly untying the gag and trying to get up. But her unsteady, shaky legs did not provide any support. Her knees met the hardwood floor, the pain ringing through her legs. She kept going on her hands and knees.

Alyson tried to rouse the others, but they were unresponsive, lost to the darkness. She stumbled and crawled toward the door, her bloody bandage trailing behind her like a gruesome banner of her suffering.

One hand in front of the other, she inched toward the door.

Her knees slid along until she reached a heavy table and pulled herself up.

Her legs were numb and unwilling.

On the table was one of the tin cups the men had used to collect the bloodletting when their bellies were full, but the crimson was still flowing. Parched and starved, she closed her eyes as she more than just contemplated the abandoned offering.

She took it into her hands, preparing to take a drink.

When she let the cup touch her mouth and the thick liquid crossed her lips, the metallic taste and thought of what she was doing made her retch.

She had to do it.

Had to build strength.

The blood seemed to help the brothers when they grew weary.

Resolve took over, and she tried again to swallow. It flowed luke-warm and heavy to her belly. She stopped to breathe.

Alyson turned back to the others as she wiped her mouth and chin. Her heart broke for them, but she had no choice. She couldn't help them in her state, but she could find someone who could.

Her eyes returned to the cup in her grasp.

She must finish it for *them*. And so, she did. Gulping their gift to her.

In mere moments, she was on the move again. Dragging herself down flights of stairs and staggering out of the building and down the street. The rising hot summer sun beat down on her and engulfed her in the weight of suffocating humidity, bright and burning her eyes.

She stumbled and fell repeatedly, her wrists throbbing with pain, but she forced herself to keep going. She was soiled and stained. No doubt smelling as putrid as her captors and the confining space that had been her prison.

As the youngster ambled and groaned further down Royal Street, receiving neither help nor eye contact from those she encountered, she spotted a beat cop holding down a vacant street corner.

She approached with overwhelming relief, tears running down her cheeks, her speech barely rising above strained whispers.

Alyson wheezed, "Help me," before falling into his arms, her tiny body nearly drained of life.

CHAPTER I
OPPORTUNITY

OUTSIDE ORLEANS PARISH PRISON, 1931

J azz music fell silent in New Orleans only three times in my mortal memory. All occasions could be attributed to something my family did. Ironic, because we had nothing, were no one, and thought even less of ourselves. But what I always had, even though I'd lost it countless times—was hope. And I couldn't live with losing it again.

The Big Easy was no stranger to violence and murder, but I remained in utter fear and disbelief upon learning of the young survivor and all those we'd fed on in the apartment, who never made it out. The city was now hunting the hunters, and getting close.

I stepped back to the shadows, pondered our fate, and rehearsed what I might reveal in interrogation while I stared at the dungeon-like confinements of the stone prison, from a safe distance. I could remember so little. Everything we'd been given was taken, most of which were our memories. Most recollections were there of our life before pulling the trigger. Before preying upon innocents. Before this macabre comedy of regret and misunderstanding, to which we, ourselves, were victims.

After all, my brother and I *were* men, not monsters.

It was ironic that our blood relations, in decades past, had escaped from the brackish backwaters and bayou, only to end up in a desolate and decaying two-block area of downtown called the Swamp. A place equally, if not more dangerous than the surrounding marshland of gators, snakes, and bull sharks. Animal nature and human nature were the same in Louisiana. Each was driven to kill or be killed. Dominate and survive. Although, leaving the bayou, my family had not actually escaped. Had their desire to find a more rewarding life been their downfall, not unlike our own?

Another flash reminiscence returned, front of mind. Would I share it?

Mother was a survivor in her own right until the night of her murder. She was Irish on her father's side. A tough family. She was the sister of a Live Oak Boys founding gang member and brothel owners John and Bill Swan. Our uncle supported our family, so Mother cleaned their Fireproof Saloon at night.

She withstood abusive and impoverished conditions to earn our keep and, during the day, delivered produce from the French Market to the Sicilian grocers who seemed to pop up overnight, claiming their own turf and turmoil in the city. Oh, how Uncle hated them so. Even through her fatigue, she taught us or found someone in the neighborhood who could. Or someone who at least would ensure we made it to the schoolhouse. She'd said what she could not provide us in luxury, we could find ourselves rich with proper speaking, writing, and maths. It was not a hard task for me, as I was a sponge to learning. Wayne, not so much.

My twin brother, Wayne, and I played together after our school lessons. He and I never looked the same. With my dark hair and long face, tutors referred to us as Pen and Pad. I, the pen, while my brother, with a blocky head of mahogany brown, the pad. After our tutoring, we ran in the shadows on dark, slippery streets laden with spilled drink, rotted food garbage, human waste, and decaying trash shrouded in sight but not smell by the two-story battered buildings. We hitched rides on the back of produce wagons going to and from the French Market. Steamship whistles cried over the rooftops to announce the readiness of their crew for nights of pleasure and self-induced oblivion on our small turf. As an escape, I took to reading by the waters, listening to waves slap against the wharf pilings. This was our kingdom, and we called it home. Even as we learned of far-away splendor, we never sought much further. Perhaps it was because we were practically each other, and that was enough, even in the squalor that it was.

Shutterless with broken windows, the look of all dilapidated structures with rotten planks on the outside was one of abandon-ment and bedlam. Inside, the floors were filled with families living in squalor and sins of the flesh and soul behind thin walls or, some-times, a simple curtain. We fit right into the broken scene, what with my fever-induced deaf ear and fainting spells. My brother with his own affliction; a mule-kicked lame knee that never slowed him down.

We dashed at night along the Mississippi waterfront port docks, liberating five-cent whiskey-filled drunken patrons from their pocket watches and monies near Archy Murphy, George Kent, and Uncle John's barroom clubs. Sure, the owners were criminals, but in our part of town, we were safe.

I would keep to myself that as we aged into our teens and whiskers grew on our cheeks and chins, we were as much a part of the petty crime and small brawls that ruled the surrounding misery. It was a wretchedness that profited from sex work, robbery, corrup-tion and extortion beatdowns. Our kingdom to defend. But my brother and I were pups among wolves, and we did not defend it well.

Perhaps they would show mercy learning we were virtually fatherless in our upbringing.

Our patriarch, Trudeau Zenon Lecartier, an accomplished trombonist but not much of a breadwinner, tried to make a more respectable living than those in our surroundings. He played his instrument, blasting and muted, entertaining patrons at all the barrooms, dance houses, Storyville whorehouses, and later, the speakeasies around town during Prohibition. He played from mid-afternoon until the late hours of the night from Exchange Alley to the South Rampart Eagle Saloon to the red-brick Iroquois and Lyric theaters. Music was the only time he raised his eyes and held his head high, bowing only to applause. It was an escape from the shame of not being able to support his family through his genuine passion. Perhaps it was why he seemed to avoid us and work harder. Time was measured by what he would provide our family in the future and less about what he could give of himself in the moment. How similar we'd become.

He was a fair-skinned Creole. Native Indian, negro, and French-Canadian. My mother's side didn't initially know about the first two. I was named John, for my uncle, in Irish guilt, she would often say.

I racked my recollections for more. Ever careful. I sought genuine memories, and not what I imagined or was later given back to remember. I no longer knew what were truths, dreams, or enduring nightmares.

Mother's family never took to Father, and even less so after her death. I suspect at least her brother suspected Father's neglect and inability to provide for his family forced my mother into the arms of another man.

When Mother went missing, a rather common occurrence, and was later discovered in the back alleyway of the Italians, authorities thought her to be a Gallatin Street prostitute who'd ended up on the better side of town. No doubt so her solicitor needn't lie in lice and the filth of sailors. Her clothes were torn near as much as her throat. Left to bleed out and feed the scavenging street vermin that gnawed at her tender flesh down to the bone.

Men working on behalf of the coroner dumped Mother's bagged-up, broken body just over the moat in the paupers' field behind the old St. Peter Street Cemetery. It was a lesser part of the disease victim Charity Hospital Cemetery, which amounted to a large trench of cloth-wrapped bodies of the poor piled upon one another. Some of Uncle's Live Oak Boys got wind of this murdered harlot's description while they searched the city for our missing mother. A small tattoo of a clover with a dagger running through it just above her breast. They probably got the information from the end of their swinging sticks as they cracked skulls for answers. Her India ink design was a telltale sign of the Live Oak Boys family, and only those in our poor corridor knew of my mother's marking to keep her safe from Uncle's clientele.

It was then, May 1918, that our father quit playing altogether, and we all went to retrieve the remains of Mother for a more proper but still not extravagant burial. He was instantly a shell of a man—if becoming lower was even possible.

As we walked the streets carrying the coffin to St. Louis Cemetery, compliments of Uncle, the clubs stayed closed. The likes of "Jelly Roll" Morton, Joe "King" Oliver, and all the other musicians marched in solidarity with their fellow band member until his wife was laid to rest. She, like others in the city, were placed short-term in the burial wall to await her family vault interment for a year and a day as the scorching Louisiana sun beat down on the tombs to decompose the bodies for the next tenant. Unlike other jazz funeral tribunals, neither the city's musicians nor my father played even one note. As common as killings were in the area, this one broke the Big Easy, as they could see it had broken my father. A man who never had the recognition of New Orleans citizens' wallets, he was one of their musical icons, taken as much for granted as a city park or the Mighty Mississippi itself.

In hindsight, I recall at the funeral an unfamiliar male voice within the small gathering say, "She was a troubled woman. Troubled indeed." He was as foreign in sound as he was in appearance to me. I did not know the man and was surprised someone of his wealthy appearance would know my mother or father. Tall, well-dressed, confident. I assumed he was a music enthusiast, as so many were in the Quarter. He certainly did not look to be a patron of my uncle's establishment. Should he have entered the Swamp with such a wealthy and smug presence, he would have been robbed or beaten before his second step.

Yet my father looked at the man and simply cocked his head in confusion. Perhaps he didn't know the man either, or struggled to recall him. Father writhed his hands as if contemplating a reply, but whatever was on his mind never passed his tongue. If the word "troubled" applied to anything, it was to Father's face.

From then on, we didn't see our father much and couldn't find him most days when we awoke. The needle, however, had found him. Boiled opium heroin became his new bride. When he occasionally made it home near daylight, he'd sleep it off, only to carry his trombone case wherever he sought his next fix until he, too, was gone.

They found Father on Wednesday morning, March 20, 1919, face down, overdosed in an alley behind Mahogany Hall in the new Red Light district. His trombone case and shoes were gone. Street rodents or dog packs had done a number on his corpse. I recall the day not so much because of his eminent death, but because the night before came a warning from the Times-Picayune newspaper in a published letter of the roaming Axe Man killer who'd filled the town with terror in the months prior. The Axe Man had taunted another attack. He claimed every person would be spared in whose home a jazz band was in full swing at 12:15; he declared "earthly time" on that Tuesday night. Those who did not jazz on the Tuesday night would get the axe. The music was in full swing. Dance halls were packed, bands and private musicians filled closed parties and homes, and no one was killed.

No one, that is, but Father.

He had murdered himself. Not with an axe. But futility.

The strange socialite who appraised my father as a "troubled man" left before I could thank him for attending the procession. Perhaps "vanished" would be a more appropriate word.

And the music stopped once more, which was when our awakening began. And we finally met Him with a more formalized introduction.

It's also when I first saw my love, Kesha Baptiste, my beacon in a vast sea of darkness, though all went from hope to Hell in the years to follow.

If I spilled all these thoughts of my life, or as much as I could safely share, could it save me?

"Is that what you want to know?" I might ask of my future captors.

And if they should prod for more, I could add, "Aside from living on the streets and begging for work and wages for nearly a decade, there's nothing more to tell. We weren't even eighteen and had less than we entered the world with."

Would an inspector lean back in his chair, balancing on the back two wooden legs, knees against the bottom of the table where my hand would rest, chained in iron manacles? Would he stroke his long sideburns with pursed lips?

The burning. The sizzling behind my eyes. Stop.

"No," he might reply. "I'd like to know about the dead bodies and dozens of other victims found in your home. Wrists slit, muscles eaten from the bone…and why your brother has already confessed, saying you two are vampires that need to be put to death."

Although, should they accuse us of demons we had become, it wouldn't quite ring true. If that were accurate, we would already be dead, which isn't the case. We are very much alive, which was how we arrived in this dire predicament at the hands of Jacques Saint Germain. They were scouring the streets for him, too.

"Oui, cher," I could say, knowing my brother would never

confess. I would have taken a small amount of control back, let it slither back my way.

And in my mind's eye, I glimpse the detective's wormy jugular vein, thumping in a rhythmic pulse that grew louder. More visible.

Thump.

Thump.

My addiction calls. My stomach churns, and my hunger erupts.

I can taste it. Taste him, thought he isn't here...or real. There is no one here in the cast off darkness of a tattered burnt out building. Its overgrown alleyway a place to be avoided by passersby. My safe haven for now.

Still, I lick my lips and fantasize about burying my face in the warmth of a gaping wound.

It's a lie. Am I mad?

I wasn't a powerful creature of the undead. I was a simple murderer from the streets and gutters of New Orleans. A failure.

An image flashed before my eyes. It was the Green Fairy. An apparition of the absinthe drink. I see, I saw? Was it now or then? The insanity that poisons me to my rotten heart and decaying mind. My mind now a self-preserving chamber of devilish thoughts.

"You've been drinking the giggle water. You're mad," I say.

"But I promise, you'll swing for what you've done. Jacques Saint Germain or not." Did I say this aloud, or would they to me upon my inevitable apprehension?

Why couldn't I remember more, and what would it take for us to turn? If only to save our necks. I tried to block my growing madness. Retrieve anything for my own secrets and sanity.

I was not a monster in my heart--or my head. Or was I from the start?

CHAPTER 2
ISOLATION

YEARS PRIOR

T
hese things I know. We had only just returned to the Swamp from Father's funeral when our uncle pulled us aside from his club, letting the remaining mourners pass and return to their state of normalcy. I heard from a distance the music starting anew. Life continues. The dead are soon forgotten.

My uncle was a rough man with an ugly history and dirty business books to match. His lavish mourner's suit and hat made him look like a man of fine schooling and respectful employment. His intent wasn't—and never was for anyone—one of condolence.

"Hold up," he said. "Pack your bags, boys. End of the line."

"Where are we going?" Wayne asked.

"There's no 'we.' Just yous. I don't want to see you around these blocks," he scoffed. "I've got a reputation to keep."

"But where shall we live? How will we live?" I asked. The same words passing from my brother's mouth as well.

Uncle wasn't interested in debate. "You had enough to pay for your father's cemetery vault. Never gave me a cent. I'm selling the place before they tear down the block. It's all moving to the district now, and Sicily's invaded and raised real estate prices. Good enough time to lessen my burden of you lot and cut my losses until I can think of a way to expand into the Quarter."

We stood gobsmacked. "You didn't pay for Father?"

"Penniless mulatto," he spat. "Aside from the last noble thing he did for me sis, I wouldn't give him the milk from a cat's teat. You'd be better off and leave your own worthless name behind, unless you can play a tune and collect on it. Lecartier is dead. What's left of his kin will die in the swamps. Shorten it. Blend in. I don't care; you can even kill yourselves. Just don't expect me to pick up the tab. Now go on. Get your things. You're out."

Wayne stiffened and stood tall, as elevated as he was able for average stature. "We can work for you." He lifted his chin, feigning the utmost confidence. "We'll join the gang."

"The Live Oaks? You two?" Uncle waved a contemptuous hand. "A book-bound weakling and a worthless gimp work for me? You couldn't even avenge your mother's death at the hand of those dirty killer dagos, much less heave a threatening branch in your fist. At least your father...well, pay no mind to that...guess you'll know in time." He winked.

"We could've taken on matters. We're tougher than we look. You could use that to your advantage," Wayne said, keeping up the bravado. "We've stolen from the docks. Gotten in fights."

Uncle sent a crushing balled fist straight into Wayne's mouth.

My brother flew back against the club wall, his head shattering the remnants of the already broken windowpane.

Uncle turned on me next, landing a phantom punch I didn't have time to see right into my stomach. The force bent me in two, stealing my breath.

Still dazed, Wayne was unrelenting. "At least give us something to get us started. You can't just turn family away like this."

"Way I see it, boys, you already owe me for a broken window.

Still think I owe you something?" Uncle questioned, his face scrunched beyond mere annoyance.

I was coughing, trying to catch my breath, when he grabbed the hair on my head through my cap, raising me to eyesight. He twisted my head to the good ear. "You think I need to give some send-off dowry to you as well?"

I shook my head.

Uncle gave a nasty chuckle. "You've always been the smarter one, John." He loosened his grip on my head and gave me a slap on the face.

I turned my head back to see Uncle had raised a pistol to my brother's chin.

"And you, boy, may not have wits, but always the stones." With a free hand, Uncle grabbed at my brother's crotch, giving it a tight squeeze. Wayne shrank. "Ask me. I dare you. Show me what you've got."

"No, Wayne," I pleaded. "Let's go."

My brother coughed from the deep, dull ache, then gritted his teeth, nodded his head, and muttered, "Yes, sir...I do."

Uncle released his grasp, spun the pistol round his finger, and handed the weapon to Wayne. "Here you are, then, lad. Your send-off gift. Tough love for the streets. Make your own fortune. Come back when the...Carter boys...have made a name of their own." He was about to turn to walk away but stopped himself. "Oh," he said as if in afterthought, which was likely not the case with street-savvy Uncle. "Did any of those musical fellows at the funeral mention a thing or two about your father's instrument and case?"

I shrugged. Nothing from me.

"Why should you care? You're rid of us," my brother fired back.

Uncle shook it off. "He owed me. I would have sold the useless thing. Let me know if it turns up around Basin Street. I'll pay you myself. Now, off and away with you."

Our own flesh and blood turned his back on us and entered the establishment, leaving his young nephews to mend broken hearts and bruised bones. For the old criminal, Father's life came down to an old, tarnished brass trombone.

Wayne stuffed the revolver into his waistband, untucked his shirt for concealment, and said simply, "Let's go, then. Time to earn our supper." He licked his swollen, bleeding lips, lapping at the drips. He wiped the rest with the back of his hand, giving it a cleaning lap as well. He rubbed the back of his head and brought forth a bloodied hand. "I'll show him. I'll make something of myself that he can never match."

I followed my brother, holding my belly, not knowing if it was from the blow or resulting queasiness of the intense sight of so much blood.

We walked for what seemed to be hours along the waterfront, cutting up town to the Central Business District, and then weaved through the neighborhoods in between. Every now and again, my eyes would focus on the bloodstain that had cascaded down the back of Wayne's neck. He gave it no further concern.

I, however, feared what others may think if they saw the fresh wound trailing like a tail from his scalp. Even those who would not meet our eyes I felt were drawn to our presence as we passed. I had an odd feeling of exposure. Of judging eyes. Of a dark presence casting its shadow upon us.

"Wayne, we should clean your bleeding," I suggested.

He licked his hand, smiled, and rubbed the back of his neck. My brother mocked me by waving his hand to me closer, then licked his fingers and wiped his neck again. He smiled. "Yum," he said. "Good meal."

Our bellies had been lean for days, even before Father's death. Mine was protesting in loud growls. Not hungry enough for what Wayne suggested in jest. At least the people we would pass until we'd found the right victim wouldn't give us a second thought. It was the first time in my life I compared myself to others in town and resented my low place in society. People had less these days, but Wayne and I had had nothing to begin with. This much was now painfully clear as my brother joked we may need to dine on our own blood.

Opportunities for fast money were scant, and with the Depression settling in, the last few months had seen fewer travelers and less frivolous drinkers with loose pockets. This was a new game we were forced to play.

Survival.

I suggested we head further uptown since dusk had passed. Perhaps we could find a rich socialite who would make an easy robbery target. Maybe a businessman stepping out from Mr. O'Brien's Club Tippery on St. Peter Street.

Within minutes, we found ourselves back on the wet cobblestone streets of the French Quarter, a misty fog settling heavily around us. The dimly lit gas lamps flickered as the growing breeze passed by, casting eerie shadows on the surrounding buildings. The scent of aged oak, moss, and sweet jasmine filled the air as if it was a potion concocted to lure us deeper than we had intended to venture.

The moon, through the wisps of expanding cloud cover, was full and bright, emitting a glow over the desolate alleyways and shuttered mansions, their balconies adorned with wrought-iron railings and intricate carvings. Distant jazz music drifted on the wind, adding a haunting melody to the already ominous atmosphere.

I still couldn't shake the feeling I was being watched, followed even, despite the absence of foot traffic. Now and then, I'd catch glimpses of shadows moving in the corners of my eyes, but when I turned to look, nothing was there. My hunger had overtaken my wits and inflicted a delirium of paranoia and hopelessness.

The eerie silence interrupted my woe-filled thoughts with the occasional creaking of old doors and shutters.

The hair on the back of my neck stood on end as we passed by an abandoned courtyard, where a large dog stood over a taken prey. Its eyes trained on us as we crossed. I strained to see whether it was a cat or rat he was eating, my animal urges envious of the fresh meat.

Pressing on, the scent of implacable decay wafted through the air, mixing with the aroma of freshly baked beignets from a nearby café, making my stomach churn even more.

"Wayne, perhaps we just find a safe, dark place and sleep. We may have more luck later, rooting through trash for something of sustenance."

My brother said nothing at first.

"I have a feeling," he spoke at last. "I think our luck is about to change. Just a bit further." Wayne pressed on. His confidence perplexed me. Darkness and doubt lurked everywhere I turned. I didn't want to press on.

Another gust of wind blew, sending a shiver down my spine, and I quickened my pace, eager to leave this otherworldly place. I'd had enough of the search for a rewarding victim. Fifty cents would buy us a poor boy sandwich and beer or bucket of crayfish and crabs. We needed little.

Wayne was the first to spot what we were hunting for. He nudged my shoulder and showed by jutting his chin.

I hadn't seen Him yet, walking in the darkest of the street shadows along the buildings as if he, too, was a part of the lightless crevices of town.

It was when He passed the gas lamp I glimpsed his tall stature raised in silhouette to the tops of the buildings he crossed. A black Homburg hat on his head added to his height. Dark vestments tailored tight to his limbs and core appeared sewn to his very skin. From his shoes shone a glimmer of reflection, their high shine giving their own periodic flicker from the lamps he passed like a cat along the brickwork and closed wooden doors. He was a carve-out in his own clouded surroundings. An ethereal presence that must have been divinely sent to us as an offering. A gift to start us in our new life. My hunger and the day's building emotion stoked rage through my veins. My heart beat faster. I wanted everything this man had, and more. I was prepared to take it all, whether he lived or died. At that moment, I did not care.

Side-eyed, I saw Wayne slide his hand toward the weapon stashed in his trousers. We were less than three to four buildings from our mark. As we slowed to ready our position and confidence, the approaching man seemed to quicken his step toward us. A bull starting his charge with a slow trot.

I swallowed hard and in an instant questioned my surety.

My hands grew wet, while my tongue dried in anticipation.

My heart pounded faster.

"Steady," Wayne whispered.

At least I thought it was a whisper. The sound was muffled beyond my affliction of deafness in the bad ear. My eyes darkened from the faint coming on.

Not now, I demanded of myself. *Don't come over me now.*

With each blink, I saw the flashes of bright stars before me. Panic was setting in. My falling sickness was making its call at a most inconvenient time. I tried to warn my brother, but it was too late.

Wayne raised the pistol toward the man. My twin commanded an order and said something I could neither hear nor recall, though it impressed upon my thoughts.

With those words, in the clouding of my senses, I remember glimpsing His eyes. Yellow, like a night predator pawing through the bayou's high grass.

I heard a shot fire.

And then another.

From the stranger's lips, that familiar voice returned to me from snapshots of the funeral encounters in my mind. I heard Him respond not from His mouth, but in my head, an explosive voice within the backdrop of feral snarls and growls that roared the word, "NEVER."

In a flurry of movement and confusion, I felt pain.

Then immediate pleasure. Pleasure I had never felt nor could ever imagine.

I fell into what I can only describe was an abyss of nothingness, but I wasn't afraid for even a moment. For I was not alone. Someone or something comforted me. Perhaps it was a dream...

CHAPTER 3
IDENTITY

I awoke in a bed of *comfort*, the likes of which I'd also never known. My head rested on a single pillow, plump and calming. The room was dimly lit. Heavy black curtains created a cocoon of darkness that blocked out any hint of streetlight or sunlight, shrouding the room in perpetual darkness. I knew not whether I had a brief spell or one that took me into the next day. The only source of illumination was a single candelabrum, flickering and casting eerie shadows upon the walls lined with bookcases, filled with dusty tomes and sorted papers that, upon first glance, could have been ancient manuscripts or old music scores. Their cracked and peeling spines, even under the low light, appeared yellowed with age.

My bed, a massive four-poster, dominated the room with its imposing presence. The sheets were white as sun-bleached bone, stark against the dark bed frame. A vanity table stood against the wall, its surface covered in an array of bottles and jars, each filled with liquids and lotions of unknown origin to the likes of me. A silver-handled brush rested atop a lace doily. I mused that the bristles may have been tangled with hair like that of Mother's, though her brush was of old splintered wood. I spotted another object in the shadows of the vanity. Dark. Metallic with dark wood. It was my brother's pistol, or one of its likeness.

Had I heard a shot fired? Two?

To clear my thoughts, I breathed in deeply and tried to gather my whereabouts. The air was thick with a musty scent, as if the secrets of the past had been trapped within its walls.

A reading chair sat in the corner, its leather seat worn, its back curved as if to cradle the occupant. It was my brother who sat in it, lifeless.

I hopped from the high mattress, pausing for a moment as my head felt light. I feared a second spell was nearing.

The floorboards creaked beneath my feet, and the sound echoed throughout the silent room, rousing Wayne to my immediate relief.

Before either of us could speak, a shadowy figure appeared in the doorway, its form large yet indistinct and hazy. As it almost glided into the room, I recognized the figure from the night before. In the low light, His complexion appeared pale, almost shining in the flame's castings.

He approached the bed, his movements fluid and graceful.

"I trust you had a restful sleep, Messieurs?" His voice was soft and calming, accompanied by a French accent, not unlike many in the Quarters, though His was much more pronounced and likely not watered by generational acceptance of the English language.

As He neared, the walls seemed to grow darker; the shadows deepening and coalescing into a thick, oppressive fog. The curtains billowed and danced as if caught in a fierce wind.

I blinked hard to align my senses.

He sauntered to the dark drapes and drew them wide, welcoming in the afternoon sunlight in which he seemed to bask, the rays appearing to pass right through Him. Then He stepped aside into the shadows.

"You've slumbered until nearly mid-afternoon. You must be famished. I know I am." He turned, with a smirk.

Despite the macabre aura his personality and form exuded, He didn't pose a threat to us in that moment.

I sat on the bed, hoping my vision and imbalance would correct itself. "I've seen you before. At both my mother and father's funeral. Did you know them?"

"But of course," he responded, as if my question was absurd. "I keep a watchful eye on the dregs and the elite. I know, or know of almost everyone in this city."

My brother was quick to follow. "And how was that acquaintance made of our parents?"

He seemed to contemplate a response for a moment, then did not reply. Instead, his nostrils flared, and he turned to the door, saying, "Enter," just as a light rap hit the wood.

The door creaked open.

The housemaid, a young woman with a light café au lait complexion and emerald green eyes that shone past small circular glasses perched upon her button nose, clutched a silver tray. It was laden with a teapot, two cups and saucers, and a plate of toast and jam.

The tray clinked as she made her way toward the enormous bed.

I moved my feet in a gesture that she could pass, needless in the abundant quarters.

"Ah, you have more manners than I would have imagined. Albeit, they could still use refinement in the lessons of being gentlemen."

My brother and I watched her every step, both ogling her presence as she passed. Her rump was plump, with the ties of her white apron hopping with each step she took. After Wayne's eyes returned to Him, mine lingered on the beautiful sight before me. She was the cleanest and smoothest-skinned woman I had ever seen. I was enchanted and longed to know her.

"Good morning, sirs," she said, barely above the sound of butterfly wings, as if in afterthought, placing the tray on the bedside table. The teapot hissed as she poured a cup of steaming hot tea, the aroma of Earl Grey filling the air, competing with the odors of all things old. She set the cup beside the plate of toast and jam, and then another, her hands shaking a little as she straightened the linen napkin.

"These boys will need more sustenance than this, I fear, Mademoiselle Baptiste. From their looks, they've been living off scraps and scavenging. Have we no meat to serve our guests?"

"No more in the house, save for what Terrance is stewing...or curing, below. Would you like me to send someone to the market, Mister Jacques? I'd be happy to go myself."

"Please have someone else. Have them prepare plenty of it. I fear the weight is too much for you to bear. The boys will stay here for a time. We must replenish our storage for them."

"As you request," she affirmed, then turned to me with a look of sadness that metamorphosed into a reassuring smile. At first I thought her politeness feigned approval despite our inconvenience, to which I was conscious-stricken of our added burden. In time, I would understand.

She left with the door opened wide and descended the grand staircase of the mansion, her footsteps echoing throughout the empty halls until I could see her no more.

The room was once again still, its occupant looming large before us.

Guests? I thought.

"As a gesture to the memories of your parents, you may stay here for a short time. I, as your...employer." He stated this as a proclamation, not an invitation. "My success allows me to take in such mutts as yourselves from time to time. Young men who would otherwise have little hope in this city to climb the social rungs and make something of themselves. The work won't be easy, mind you, lest everyone would be at the top."

"And what work would you have us do?" Wayne asked. "Is it... Mister Jacques?"

"Indeed," He replied. "How rude of me not to introduce myself after I was nearly robbed by you hooligans. Jacques St. Germain." He gave a dramatic, slight bow. "Future heir to the Compte St. Germain, friend and advisor to French royalty...and now, yourselves." He turned to the door with a bit of the same flair. "As for the work? I'll think of something...suiting...and interesting."

"And what if we can't do it?" I burst, without a thought.

"Ah, there it is. From the gutter, it is hard to see the view. I promise you may not even know you're doing it." His grin was coy and foretelling, though we did not yet know.

Mr. Jacques had already defined us in his mind and stinging words. A truth of our place in this world that we could not escape on our own. The offer seemed too good to pass. We'd hoped for success in crime and were afforded genuine opportunity.

I beamed with joy. *How lucky were we?*

As Jacques left our room, I stood and quickened to the window.

It was bolted shut; the panes, at closer look, were smeared with dust and grime, as if no one had opened them in decades. The wooden frame was scratched deep and throughout, as though an animal was determined to let itself out with desperate clawing.

Below us, I recognized the cobblestoned view of Royal Street. We were still in the heart of the French Quarter.

The question was, were we truly employed guests? Or, given the condition of the window, were we prisoners?

Wayne came to my side, resting his hand on my shoulder. He whispered to my ear, "I shot him twice, and yet here He stood." Realizing my brother had spoken into my deaf side, Wayne moved to my other.

I touched my bad ear, realizing his mistake but hearing all he said.

I tilted my ear. "Say something again."

CHAPTER 4
COMPASSION

"Helloooo," Wayne called into my bad ear, his eyebrows raised in anticipation.

I waved my arms, excited as a child with candy.

"John, how is this possible?" He gave a jump and paced around the room in celebratory bewilderment as he realized his own miracle had occurred.

The entire experience of awakening with insignificant memory and the imposing welcome by our host had caused Wayne to disregard his own healing. His leg was now nimble and free from chronic pain.

"Did He give us a foreign elixir?" he mused. "Perhaps something from those strange bottles on the stand?"

We were in Heaven. The two of us scoured the room for clues while devouring the food set before us, grinning from ear to ear.

Still, as strangers in this grand home, we were reluctant to cross the invisible transom from our room to the rest of the house. There was no barrier, but we were not about to test our luck and find ourselves back on the street before learning more of our fantastical gifts.

We waited patiently, chatting among ourselves about what our job could be, who this man was, and whether we had met good fortune with a second chance or whether danger would soon befall us with the host simply stalling for the authorities to arrive. The latter, we hoped not to be true.

The beautiful servant returned within the hour with an enormous silver platter of cut sausages, cooked meats, and breads.

Our eyes met as she placed the bountiful meal before us. She turned quickly and headed for the door.

"Wait," I pleaded, not knowing exactly what I would say but knowing my heart could hardly let her go.

She stopped politely.

"My name is John. This is my twin brother, Wayne. May I know your name?"

She pursed her lips, eyes darting from side to side.

I wondered whether she was shy or if my talking to the help would land her in trouble. "Surely you, as a free woman...we can speak to one another. I, myself, am part Creole."

"Mmmtooo," Wayne mumbled, his mouth stuffed with food.

"I assure you, we're men of kind hearts. There's no reason to fear us. I hope Mr. Jacques didn't share our simple misunderstanding last night. We could hurt no one."

Wayne chided with a swallow, "My brother isn't feared by anyone in the whole of New Orleans."

He laughed.

I reddened.

She smiled.

I gushed.

Wayne blew raspberries at the sight. "Oh, this is just painful to watch." He attacked our second meal, leaving me to tend to my awkwardness.

"I should go," she said. "Please let us know if there is anything further you need during your stay. Monsieur Jacques will have clean...well, new clothes for you soon. And a hot bath. He'll expect you downstairs early this evening. You'll be called upon."

I stepped closer to her, careful not to cause alarm.

She, in response, shuffled toward the door, her eyes and head low.

"I'd very much like to know your name, should you be willing to share it?" I quivered with anxiety, closed my eyes, and said what I was thinking, careful to lower my voice so Wayne, and possibly she, could not hear it. "I'm sure your name is as beautiful as you."

Her head lifted, and her eyes rose to mine.

Wayne gaffed, his mouth filled with meat, cheese, and bread.

Still, she said nothing until she turned and walked out the door. "Kesha. Kesha Baptiste."

The housemaid hurried down the staircase, as if chased by an unspeakable fear I attributed to our smell and lowly class.

"Was it us, or does she know something we should?" I asked my brother.

"You fret way too much."

"She's a young girl who is supposed to be working, and you are on one knee, practically asking for her hand."

I was overcome by puppy love, it was true, but I still sensed something was terribly wrong in our room or the house, and there was something she dared not speak of to anyone. But what did I know? I knew nothing of women at my age, not for lack of want.

Our answer neared as time ticked on.

As Ms. Kesha had promised, we were led by a houseman,

Terrance, to quarters where we could change and bathe. He provided us brief instructions on navigating the knobs, dials, lotions, and soaps. Either he'd been informed or could read on our faces that we'd never witnessed such opulence. He directed us with restrained amusement.

Our bodies cleaned and hair parted, we then donned the formal dining pants and jackets laid before us, each a perfect fit. Soon, we were summoned to come down. At least we both thought we had heard the calling from Mr. Jacques but could not be sure, even with both of my ears in working order. We had so many questions.

Terrance awaited us before our descent. Tall and unassuming, he was as discreet and accommodating as Kesha. He fixed our ties and straightened our jackets. He flattered us with departing words of encouragement. His last words were, "Be strong. And don't sweat the things you will never remember." He bid us goodbye and hurried down the steps to his next task.

The staircase in the Royal Street mansion was the centerpiece of the grand hall, with its ornate rail carvings and wrought iron spindles winding up to the second floor. We, dressed in the finest evening attire we had ever seen, much less worn, made our way down the steps, the sound of our fine leather shoes clicking and echoing with each step sending me beaming. Wayne, too, was nearly overcome by an unknown sense of pride.

"We've done it," he beamed. "We're our own men. We're the Carters, brother. After tonight, we could be legends," he joked.

As we reached the bottom of the staircase, we were greeted—and shocked — by the sight of a lavish evening party. Socialites, all dressed in the latest fashion, mingled and chatted, sipping champagne and nibbling on canapes. I was surprised to see trays of headless shrimp, crayfish and crab in mounds without shell or smell.

We wore the proper clothes for the affair but were way out of our element.

"Are we to serve them?" Wayne whispered to me as our prideful gallop slowed to a shy shuffle. His face wore disappointment and concern.

We should have known better. We were the dregs Jacques had referred to. Those who serve but are never served.

The room was dimly lit, with the ever-present candlelight flickering on the walls and chandeliers casting a warm glow over the scene. My nose filled with the thick scent of expensive perfume, cigars, and the tantalizing aroma of the feast to come. Or that we would plate for the guests.

We hadn't eaten this much over months, and I wondered if we would eat at all this evening.

Waved to come by our host, we made our way through the throng of posh guests, exchanging awkward pleasantries and avoiding eye contact as we traversed the small crowd. These people were well-known individuals in the social circles of New Orleans, and their presence was always eagerly expected at events such as this. We didn't actually know this. Their confidence oozed this truth.

What could Wayne or I even say about ourselves if asked?

Reaching Mr. Jacques, He shook our hand vigorously, then announced that the guests should make their way to their seats around the immense table. The conversation died down, and all eyes turned to us standing together, not knowing what to do next. It was as if we were the special guests of this grand affair and everyone was eager to see what surprises we had in store for their amusement.

Wayne whispered, "Should we have brought a trombone?"

I pressed my lips in restraint to at least pretend to be proper and mannered.

The night was still young, and the air was charged with the electricity of the unknown—our own anticipations.

Jacques affirmed to us, "The guests are all eager to see what you have in store for them. This will truly be a night to remember...if you can."

Wayne boasted, "With all this in our reach, how could we forget?

Thank you, Jacques." My brother's smile spread as wide as the vast table.

"Enjoy yourselves and your service to our guests. Let the first of your work begin."

Jacques wrapped His arms around our shoulders as we stood facing the guests. He kissed us both on the cheeks.

"Have you ever seen a fairy?" He asked, with an impish smirk.

CHAPTER 5
INDULGENCE

As we stood with Jacques, awaiting our purpose or invitation to do who knows what, Miss Kesha wheeled a serving table into the room. Upon it, bottles and glasses. It seemed like dessert preparation, although I wondered why it would be before the meal was even served. Terrance followed and nodded to Mr. Jacques, who clapped and hurried over.

"Gentlemen," he addressed me and my brother. "Tonight, your work will be in joining us for a celebration of ourselves. A welcoming of sorts to your new life as guests under my roof, on your journey to greatness and power."

Wayne and I recognized at least a few of the bottles. Our smiles faded. My brother and I knew little about high society affairs, but being raised in taverns and brothels, we knew absinthe and to stay away from the potent drink.

Whiskey, gin, and rum were our poisons, even at our young age. However, we didn't dare refuse our host. We were still learning our purpose and didn't want to offend. Each encounter should have told us more yet only raised more curiosity under the spell of extravagance that threw all caution to the wind.

Absinthe was a rather iconic liquor with a potent and notorious reputation. While most patrons in the Swamp drank it straight, I soon saw that in these circles, preparing and serving the drink was a ritualistic and carefully crafted process that involved fancy tools and techniques.

Kesha retrieved from the lower shelf of the cart a glass Pontarlier, which she placed on the table. She placed a slotted spoon with a flat bottom on top of the glass. A sugar cube was then placed on the spoon, and a healthy measure of absinthe was poured over the sugar.

The liquor was then set on fire, and as the sugar caramelized, cold water was dripped slowly, louched over the sugar cube, and into the absinthe. The drink turned cloudy and milky. Terrance conducted the same cocktail ceremony on adjacent tables.

Kesha was about to stir the mixture when Mr. Jacques instructed her to wait.

"We forgot the most special ingredient," he announced, with his usual flair and ceremony.

From the copper goblet in his hand, our host added to the mixture his own drink contents.

Wayne and I looked with unease as what we assumed must be wine was much thicker as it poured and the last remnants dripped.

"What the devil?" Wayne whispered.

Mr. Jacques turned to him, his smile dropping to a disappointed scowl. "Correction, Mr. Carter. You'll sup on the Devil's *Fairy,* and she will fly and dance about you, waving her magical dust over your...inhibitions."

Our host poured from the bottles a similar red liquid into the white mixture, blending it further in the glass to a dark pink color. He offered the first glass to my brother. "Drink. Drink deep. For tonight, this is your first task."

Wayne, always ready to step to a challenge, did as he was instructed, without the slightest pause.

I had grown nauseous and planned to refuse politely. My eyes returned to the spoon and the white substance that had burned. In my mind's eye, I could see my father and the substances he burned and injected.

Yes, said a voice in my head. It wasn't Him. It was someone else. *My father?* I thought. I knew it wasn't sugar. *Run, John. Run,* the voice kept telling me. *Lest you wish to wake like us.*

When a glass was offered to me, the voice within my mind said no, but my hand accepted, and soon the bitter herbal and iron taste, hinting of sweet anise, cooled my throat, followed by a slight sting, and in an instant the cup was empty.

Kesha winced as my eyes turned from the drink to her stare. A small tear welled upon her lower lid and then fell.

I was so moved by her concern that my senses fired to their utmost. I could have sworn I heard the single tear splash when it glided down her cheek and hit the floor.

She turned to leave, and I heard a soft voice, barely audible in the room's stillness. It was Him.

"Thank you, Miss Kesha. I trust that you'd join were it not for your...other dutiful obligations." He smiled with his unwavering charm and turned back to the party, not waiting for a reply.

She shuddered. From my vantage point, which focused like the sight of a hawk, I watched as her skin rose, prickling with fear. I reached my hand out, yearning to touch and comfort her.

A hand touched my flesh. My head spun to Mr. Jacques, whose eyes appeared even more sunken and dark, his flawless skin in the candlelight ashen and waxy. "Never mind the help," he said to me. His attention was now on the parade of women entering the room. They wore Venetian masks, and little more. Nubian men weighed with heavy muscular physiques, accompanied them, clapping as they wound through the guests. These men, too, had little in their coverings, save for a mask and modest silk loin cloths that moved in the rhythm of their gait.

"Ah," our host leered. "Compliments of la France and l'Afrique, who continue to send only the most beautiful and strongest of their country and continent. Thank you to my trading partners and dear late friend, Messier La Moyne," he announced in an almost hypnotic voice, his eyes darting about, though locking for a moment upon everyone's, making each word he spoke personal. "Lads," he lowered his voice in a whisper to us, "Among these fine ladies, you may sample the prestigious women of Le Petit Salon, should you grace them stories of adventure...and a stallion's mast," he nudged, encouraging us to mingle.

Wayne's hand grabbed my wrist and pulled.

I turned to him but was fixated on Kesha.

A small stream of smoke rolled from her tongue. From where it came, I hadn't a guess. As the smoke escaped her mouth, rose, and circled around her head, a strange voice passed from her luscious lips.

CHAPTER 6
PURSUIT

At first, I thought the trails of smoke or vapor escaping her mouth were just my imagination. Somewhere between my drink, this strange place, and the overwhelming presence of strangers from an influential society well above my stature, I was not myself. As I watched, suspicious of the rising apparition, the white cloud rose gently in a spiral up the grand room's ceiling. A stream wafted to me and circled my head. I'd expected the acrid scent of tobacco and bitterness it might taste on my tongue. Instead, the sweet smell of jasmine filled my nostrils.

I inhaled and lifted another drink of absinthe to my lips. How another glass came into my hands was a less important mystery. The anise taste was overpowering the metallic bitterness of the unfamiliar cocktail ingredient that had its own distinct flavor. As I took another sip, I experienced a greater burn, yet not of alcohol, as it clawed down my throat. Something else, strange; the aftertaste lingered in a tingle on my tongue, spreading to small pinpricks on my face.

The smoke regained my attention. It seemed to have a life of its own, twisting and turning in the air as it climbed higher and higher.

The tendrils reached up towards the ornate moldings, as if trying to escape the confines of the room.

The smoke seemed to wrap around everything, clinging to the furniture and walls. I found myself strangely captivated by its movements. It was as if the smoke was trying to tell me something, to reveal a hidden message in its swirling patterns. It waved to me, gesturing for me to come closer.

I followed.

As I looked closer, I saw the unmistakable form of a small fairy flitting about the room. She flew from gossamer wings and exuded a mystical glow that seemed to emanate from within. I fixated on her delicate dance around me. Perhaps the absinthe unlocked something deep within my mind, allowing me to see the hidden things.

She soared toward my brother. Wayne also appeared nervous and excited about the turn this party had taken, and the literal magic in the air.

I felt as though my mind was floating with the vapor. As the minutes passed, I had a strange sense of detachment from my surroundings. The room seemed to shift and change around me, and the colors seemed more vibrant and intense. I watched the scene from above, witnessing me and my brother mingling effortlessly with the other guests, our readings and lessons paying off as our words were as silken as their white gloves and kerchiefs.

Despite my confusion, I became drawn to the charming socialites. They seemed to understand me and made me and my `brother I feel welcome. They were all so beautiful. I made romantic advances towards both men and women, unable to resist their intoxicating allure, though I struggled to remember their names and details of our conversations. None of it really seemed to matter.

As the night wore on, my hallucinations grew more vivid. I saw strange, bright colors and patterns dancing before my eyes. The pain and pleasure seemed to blend into an overwhelming, dizzying sensation as we shed our garments. My memory lapses became more frequent, and I felt disoriented and out of place. Jacques sawed on a violin, his erratic movements that of a devil on fire. The room spun, and I found it hard to focus on anything or anyone. I started laughing uncontrollably at inappropriate moments, drawing amusing looks from the other guests who touched and caressed me with reassurance and interest.

Despite the surreal nature of the experience, I felt oddly comforted by the tiny fairy's presence as the night drifted on. She seemed to embody all the beauty and magic of the world, and I felt privileged to have been granted a glimpse of her realm. The green fairy had shown me a side of life I had never known before, and that I longed to see more of.

She drew closer, could have perched on my nose. I was exhilarated.

"Speak to me," I said, "That I may know your name."

"Why, you know my name," the fairy replied, growing in size and clenching my arms. "It's Jacques."

I felt a sudden shock of recognition as the name hit me like a bolt of lightning.

Jacques.

The name seemed to echo through the room, bouncing off the walls and ringing in my ears. It was a name I had heard before, but I couldn't remember where or when.

Jacques.

JACQUES.

Was there one of them, or two?

The echo in my mind faded to silence and ease returned as I sunk deeper into my chair.

The fairy, now larger and grown to human size, continued to speak. Her voice was gentle and melodic, filling me with warmth and light. She told me of a magical world that existed beyond our own, a realm where anything was possible and dreams could become a reality.

As I listened, my excitement morphed into a growing sense of unease in the pit of my stomach. Something about her story didn't seem quite right, and I couldn't shake the feeling that there was more to her tale than she was letting on.

I felt more hands on me.

Smelled the scent of musk and perfume.

The smell of absinthe and cigars on the lips of those I embraced.

Then the room grew dark. The lights flickered and then went out completely, plunging the grand room into pitch blackness. I was floating in darkness without an anchor, unable to hear or see anything. Panic set in.

Then I heard a whisper in my ear. It was the fairy's voice, but it sounded different now - deeper, contorted, and filled with malice.

"Welcome to my world," she said, and I could feel her hot breath on my skin.

I tried to scream, but no sound would come out. My arms felt glued to my sides, my limbs like cement. It took all my strength and focus to keep breathing.

Breath in, two, three, four...

And out, two, three, four...

I kept counting. All I could do was count to keep myself alive.

Then, just as suddenly as it had come, the darkness lifted, and the lights flickered back on.

I looked around the room, disoriented and confused. The other guests stared at me with hungry eyes, some behind masks.

My brother, too, wore one of white porcelain. The rounds of the eyes were dark. Painted features, demonic.

"What happened?" I asked, my voice trembling. "What is that?"

No one had an answer.

They drew closer, and someone handed me another drink.

I swallowed it fast. And then, I saw something move in the corner of my eye. It was the fairy, still flitting about the room, her delicate wings beating faster and faster. I could feel her watching me, studying me as if she was waiting for something.

I knew then I had to get out of the mansion, I had to leave before it was too late. Soon it would be too late! I stumbled towards the door, my mind reeling with confusion and fear.

As I stepped outside into the cool night air, I felt a sudden wave of relief. The world seemed to snap back into focus, and my senses returned more clearly once again; the street lamps along the street, the jazz in the air. I lifted my head to the sky, just for a moment, and took a deep breath.

The hands fell upon me once again. It was Jacques, and Jacques, and the fairy.

They drew me back to the lurid festivities, while the fairy giggled her heavenly laugh.

CHAPTER 7
CYCLE

I woke up in a strange but familiar, dimly lit bedroom, my head pounding and mouth dry. As I looked around, I realized I was in a large, ornate gathering room and not alone on the floor, covered with plush cushions, furs, blankets...and bodies. I was no longer in the Swamp.

From the candlelight glowing in all corners of the vast parlor, I could see several other people sleeping beside me. From what little I could make out, all of them were strangers, but something about them felt familiar. I couldn't quite place it, but I had a nagging sense of déjà vu. Never could I have recalled such a scene, even under the roof of a brothel for so many years as a child. This was not normal.

I slowly begin pulling myself up, trying to shake off the grogginess. The scent of incense, smoke, and seamy sexual redolence wafted through the strange sight and smells. The furniture was ornate, the wood dark and rich, with heavy velvet curtains draped over the windows and tapestries adorning the walls.

I tried to recall how I got here, but my memory was hazy. The last thing I remembered was...leaving a funeral...my uncle...a dark stranger my brother and I intended to rob, but everything was a blur after that.

My brother. Wayne. Where was he? Where was I?

As I tried to gather my thoughts, one of the people closest to me, a woman, stirred, and I realized they were all waking up, too. All around me, naked bodies began to stretch and rouse like a soft earthquake. They looked at me groggily, and then their eyes widened in surprise. No one, including my brother and me, in the room was clothed.

"Hey, you're here, too?" the comforting voice of my brother said, sounding confused. I turned to find him splayed across a long sofa. He was not alone and just as surprised as I was.

I nodded, sharing his bewilderment. As the other people in the room woke up, I began to understand they all seemed to know each other, but from overhearing their conversations, none could remember how they got there. None but Wayne and I seemed to care.

The head of a young, bespectacled Creole woman peeked around the corner. Even from the distance of the room and haze in my head, I could tell she was beautiful. My soul reached out to her like it knew her, but I could not place the face, no matter how much her lovely radiance pulled my heart her way.

She lowered her eyes and rushed toward me, fabrics in her arms, navigating the ground of Bacchus nudity covering the floor.

Modest and exposed, I attempted to cover myself while witnessing the most alluring creature come toward me in awe.

She took a deep breath with a heavy, accompanying exhale. "You're safe, John. Don't be afraid."

"How do you know my..."

"Quick," she said, tossing garments to both me and my brother. "Put these on while He sleeps."

"Where are we?" I asked, groggy, my limbs unresponsive.

"The same place you have been for months. Now hurry."

"Months?"

Wayne made no attempt at catching the clothes. Instead, he nuzzled closer to the brunette woman in his arms. "I'm not going anywhere."

I looked to him, and then to the lovely lady coaxing me to flee by her side. "I don't even know you?"

"John, it's me. Kesha. Please try to think. If you still love me," she said, eyes welling with tears and a look of desperate concern. "I'm begging you."

"Love?" I was dismayed but not altogether unwilling. "Have we not just met?" Still, the way my heart pulled from my clouded reasoning, I felt the need to trust her.

"Wayne, will you not come?" I asked my brother.

"Why would I? There's no danger." The woman in his arms cooed and started kissing his bare chest. He turned to me with a smile, his eyes dark and reflecting a flicker of the dying candles. "I'll never leave."

His brunette companion straddled him as she continued her path of licking and lip-smacking his neck. She rocked in rhythmic motions, moaning as she buried her face further under his chin. He groaned in a moment of pain that turned to rapture.

Kesha continued to pull me with unrelenting intensity. "At least escort me to the market. Can you please do that? Just a walk. A simple morning walk through the Quarters. A stop at Cafe du Monde."

I contemplated what seemed reasonable enough. "But we will return? I can't leave my brother." I glanced back at him with concern, but he seemed to have forgotten anyone else was around as his passions grew. Others in the room renewed their own carousals.

"Yes." Kesha nodded, biting her lower lip. "We'll come right back."

My brother appeared to be in capable hands, so how could I resist?

CHAPTER 8
BREAKING

Miss Kesha took my hand as soon as I was dressed and rushed me out of the mansion.

My eyes and chest burned from the bright morning and humid air that filled my lungs. I tried to slow down, but this lovely yet unfamiliar woman rushed me through the streets as I reacquainted myself with surroundings I had known but never recognized with such brilliance; the sights and sounds of the French Quarter. The smell, while not pleasant, was interesting in its own way. It was as if I could discern the unique aroma of every element discarded on the streets and walkways as we weaved through pedestrians and trash.

Kesha's pace quickened as we turned down Dumaine Street.

I was certain we had been running for minutes, but my breath was full, even in the summer heat.

"Here," she said, nudging me to an alley opening, which blossomed into a lovely courtyard.

No time to admire. I was jerked again toward a narrow connecting path between two brick storefronts, then pulled into a dark opening with a flickering gas lamp and small painted sign with

46

the writing *Mama Loca Tea and Biscuits*. Kesha stepped toward an ornately hand-carved, paneled door that opened with hardly a push.

I looked to Kesha for answers.

"Mama Loca is my aunt."

Disappointed but not angry, I followed.

Upon entering this hidden parlor, we found ourselves in a small foyer decorated with various curiosities. Skulls, crystals, bones, which I assumed must be from an animal. The walls were painted a dark red, with symbols and designs brushed on top. A faint but pleasant scent of incense, or perhaps herbs, permeated the air, mingling with the smell of candles and food stewing from another room.

Still gripping my hand, Kesha guided me through a beaded curtain to a larger chamber. My eyes rose to the high ceiling. I could not fathom what building I had entered from the streets. Again, I was smitten by the elaborate decorations and moody lights casting shadows around us. The place felt sacred. Maybe a little dangerous.

The room's center was filled with a round, raised platform. Not a table, though it had chairs and large cushions about. The walls were covered with tapestries and paintings depicting battles and religion, dancing, and signs of the heavens.

Cabinets lined the lower half of the walls, containing grimoires, herbs, and other esoteric paraphernalia.

A tall woman approached from a dark corner. Her presence startled me. I thought I'd heard the breathing and beat of a heart.

"Why have you come here, child?" she asked Kesha.

"He's being tested," she said, with concern.

"The darkness is plenty. Desperation. Danger to you."

"I need him to see," Kesha pleaded.

"Need? Want? Leave him."

"I can't."

I did not know it at the time, but the old woman was a Sangoma shaman. She wore long swaths of colorful patterned fabrics that covered her head and had a distinctive hairstyle of red dreadlocks shaped in a mushroom on her head. Her head cocked, and after an uncomfortable pause, she said, "Welcome, Mr. John."

"How do you know-"

She raised a hand, bidding me to speak no further. "John Lecartier," the shaman said. She directed her full attention to Kesha. Mama Loca's eyes rolled back to their whites. The conversation started anew, but in another deeper voice coming from the shaman's mouth. "You have brought him to me. Why, child?" The shaman spoke while gathering various items from the shelves and resting them on the center table.

Miss Kesha started, "He needs-"

"I know what he needs, child. Why have you left your ancestors? Why have you stirred Mr. Jacques's distrust? He cannot know if you are to be safe."

Kesha frowned. "I'm watching over the dead in that horrible place. They don't speak to me. No one does. No one but John and Mr. Terrance."

"Your time is not complete. There are others raising danger. You must stay. Mr. John must stay. Do I not protect and heal your soul while you are there?"

"You do not know what happens behind closed doors. Good men like John and his brother are in danger. I'm trying to stop it."

"Mr. John was in danger long before he came to the home of Mr. Jacques. Doors do not hide what I know to be between the living and the dead. To be the test. To fall into the treachery of the Way."

"I do not understand," I interjected, finding my lost voice, wishing to understand why I was brought here instead of the marketplace.

Mama Loca frowned. "Too many words. Words you will not understand until you can see. Can remember." Her head snapped in my direction. "Sit," the voice demanded.

"But I-"

"SIT," she ordered.

I did as instructed, as did Kesha. I don't know what made me think I had any say in what was about to happen.

Mama Loca fiddled with jars and cloth wrappings. "You have been bewitched by what shall not be named. Sage," she said as she dropped leaves and stems into a bowl. "Rosemary and my blend of herbs." She poured oil and then lit a long stick, which she waved in the air, pointed to all corners of the room, then dropped into the mixture, which sizzled and sputtered as the flame grew. She placed a small mirror on the table that faced me and lit a candle before it.

As the flames in the bowl grew, she covered it with a purple cloth, then lifted a small opening, breathing in the smoke, which she blew into my face.

I coughed.

"Breathe it in; fill your soul." She repeated the process. I followed her orders.

A sharp pain exploded in what felt like the center of my head. I shrieked.

"Look to the mirror."

In the reflection, I saw the image of Mr. Jacques. I gasped in horror. His eyes were yellow. That night. I remembered.

"Now say your name to the mirror, to Mr. Jacques. Say it until you see yourself."

She blew more smoke into my face. I said my name. Again. Again. I felt the hand of Kesha rest on my shoulder.

Slowly, in the reflection, the face morphed like a ripple in water and turned into my own.

"Your hand, Mr. John. Give it to me."

I reached across the table, my arm extended, hand open.

Mama Loca slid a long knife across my palm before closing it to a fist. Then she hovered my hand over the embers of her offering, letting the droplets of blood drip.

Like the curtains drawing to open a moving picture show, I saw my life over the past days, weeks, perhaps months, as I had been told by my love. Kesha. Stolen moments with her. Moments stolen from me by strangers with greedy hands. A barbaric intimacy. Pain. Pleasure. Those eyes. Those yellow and sometimes red eyes. They followed me everywhere. A voice speaking to me, whispering to me. Laughter. The blood. Oh, the blood. Our bodies were bare and writhing with others as offerings, and victims were slain and loved. The moments flooded my mind, transforming from something I watched to something I remembered. I was there. And all the while, so too was Kesha to cleanse me, hold me, and comfort me as I wept.

I was present once more and turned to my beloved. For the moment, I remembered. Remembered it all. I wept again in shame and frailty. What had me in such a spell? In that instance, I knew it was Him.

"He's back," Kesha said to her aunt. "Can you protect him, Aunty?"

"Mr. Jacques will know."

"I must help my brother and bring him to you," I pleaded to Mama Loca.

Again, with the wave of a hand and ticking of a long, bony finger. "There is still much work to do, Mr. John." Mama Loca opened a small bottle. In it were strands of hair and fingernails. She walked to the corner of the room, lifted something large, hefted it over to the table, and unbuckled the metal clasps. I recognized it immediately when she opened the case. My father's trombone. She flipped over a compartment that held the lower slide of the instrument. Flipping it over exposed yet another opening. In it was an axe. The axe of the Axe Man?

As I stared in disbelief, she poured the spirit bottle contents into the bowl.

"There is grave danger coming to you and your family's name by the hand of another." Her voice, now returned to her own, carried through the room, pulling me away from my father's sole and lost possession. "You may be forced to spill the blood of innocents. Speak to your father, Mr. John. He has much to tell. Know Miss Kesha is to be trusted above all. The rest you must forget, so you can save your soul. Or Jacques will know. They will all know. Jacques is just a man, but a powerful man kissed by the Knights of Hell. Beware of such a kiss unto you."

CHAPTER 9
POSSIBILITY

Thinking back, I don't know how much I recalled of the curious session with Mama Loca. I remember leaving as another man sought to enter her establishment. The gentleman and I exchanged brief pleasantries, but as I passed, I felt his eyes remain on me until Kesha and I turned back into the maze-like catacombs of nestled buildings.

A RECOUNTING of Eddie

In the months since the last Axeman murder, few had forgotten the fear, as well as the fact that the killer remained at large. Among them was Ernest Toussaint, or Eddie the Glove, as he was called by folks in the Quarter. Eddie the Glove was one of the first policemen of color in New Orleans. His name was familiar to many, but not to I, until I had met him or heard a later recounting.

While he carried a firearm when he was on duty, Eddie's weapon of choice was a pair of leather gloves sewn together, stitched with sand packed inside them. It didn't take long for a reputation of firm fairness and thought-provoking cowhide beatdowns to award Eddie the Glove the respect he deserved.

But as Jim Crow laws and antebellum southern social order came about, retirement spread rampantly across the state as pervasive and visible as Spanish moss. He'd achieved high commendations and an award from the mayor for his detective work in a city of darkness and violence known for unsolved murders, particularly in the French Quarter. The police department had been understaffed and over-whelmed, and many crimes went unsolved until they gave Eddie a shot.

Up to the point of being put out to pasture with a modest retire-ment, he'd seen more than his fair share of violence and investigated countless murders, seeing the worst that humanity offered. Upon retirement, he tried settling into a quiet life in the French Quarter but couldn't shake the feeling that he was destined to do more, that his work wasn't done. He had always been a man of action and couldn't stand to see innocent people hurt. The Axe Man murders drew him back to the streets. With a small notebook in one of his pockets and his gloves tucked into the back of his waistband, he meandered through the riverside neighborhood as if it were his own beat.

One night, while walking the last legs of his self-imposed city watch, Eddie stumbled upon a small team of men in an alley. It looked like an unwanted sexual encounter, so the old cop crept along the dark enclave shadows while freeing his heavy gloves for action. Close enough to stop the assault and ensure the men didn't run off, Eddie gave a shout before springing to action. As he committed to his own attack, his limbs froze in horror. The gang was feeding on a young woman. He had heard rumors of such creatures in the Quarters before but never truly believed them.

The creatures scattered, not in fear, but to surround him in a counter maneuver. He swung at them as they swarmed, though his efforts were futile. He was engulfed by clawing hands. One lunged at Eddie and sank its teeth deep into his neck. Through the pain, he drew his revolver and fired at the blood-lusting monsters.

It was the sound, not the impact they feared. The shot echoed through the silent night.

Eddie was left for dead but didn't die. Instead, he awoke several hours later in the care of Mama Loca.

It was Mama Loca whose counsel he sought this very morning as he wound through her secretive entrance, entered her sacred domicile, and stood patiently as she held the head of a puff adder, a highly venomous viper, in her mouth. From what Eddie later told us, she performed a slow, trance-like dance as the snake coiled around her neck. Her arms twirled, outstretched, feathers in each hand waving in simulated flight. At its conclusion, she removed the snake and placed it in a straw basket where the offering of a white rat awaited.

Unfazed by Eddie, she removed her animal skin coverings for a long yellow dress. "You have not asked but wish to know. He was here to visit me," she said, dry and unaffected. "They want him. The young man and his brother, Mr. Ernest."

"Always a step ahead. Where is he now? No one has seen the boys in months."

"He lives with Him."

"Is he one of them yet?"

"He is neither the living nor the dead."

"Hmm. Being groomed?"

"New Or-lee-ans not safe for the dead. And undead. They need gris-gris and blood thieves so they can stay in the shadows."

"Speaking of..." Eddie sat at the large circular table and rolled up his shirt sleeve.

Mama Loca gave an affirming nod, then retrieved from a sideboard a small jar and three long apothecary vials. These she placed next to a wooden cup.

"They look fat," he said, looking at the jar of belly-full leeches.

The healer retrieved the blood slugs one by one, giving a gentle but firm squeeze until they'd given up their bloody bounty. She returned each to the jar, that they may feed and host again.

"What would I do without the pharmacist and barber making their donations?"

Mama Loca only gave a small nod as she continued her work. Next was the pouring of vials into the cup. "It may make you feel weak at first. The barber, Mr. Thomas, he transfused an ailing old man of his liver sickness."

This time, it was Eddie who delivered the small nod of understanding. Their weekly ritual had been as such since the attack.

When Mama Loca finished filling the cup, she produced her own jar. Empty. She lifted a thin rubber hose from a wooden box and wrapped it tightly around Eddie's bicep. Also within the container was a syringe.

"Give before you take," she said, piercing his arm and starting the flow into her container.

She finished, and upon withdrawing the steel needle from his arm, the small puncture wound closed.

"Now?" Eddie asked for permission.

"Now," she said.

He guzzled from the cup with greed. As he did so, his eyes glowed as his dark pupils shrunk and iris expanded, turning a bright yellow hue.

Mama Loca smiled. "The good hunter returns."

CHAPTER 10
GUILT

K esha and I dropped our clasped hands in unison as we turned onto Royal Street and neared Jacques's house, me feeling a pit of apprehension in my stomach. I had left without permission, and now I was worried I'd be reprimanded. Had I broken one of the house rules that had never been spoken of nor implied? Would I be in trouble?

Kesha urged me not to be concerned if she could speak first and assure Jacques we were at the market...and *only* the market.

I walked up to the door and tried to conjure an excuse for why I had left without consent if Jacques pressed. True, we had gone to the market to get groceries, and it sounded plausible enough. I just hoped Jacques would believe me.

I twisted the unlocked knob just as Jacques opened the way. He looked surprised to see me, or so it appeared.

"John, is everything okay?" He asked.

Kesha nudged up. "We were at the market, Monsieur Jacques."

He nodded in understanding and turned to me.

I took a deep breath and said, "Yes, Mr. Jacques, everything's fine. We just went to the market to get some groceries."

Jacques's eyebrows furrowed. He extended a hand and touched my neck.

I bristled but allowed His gentle grasp. He eyed me suspiciously.

"Your heart is racing. Concerned that I don't approve of your freedom? Or that of Miss Kesha's?"

He dropped His hand but remained standing in the door frame, blocking our passage.

I felt my heart sink. Had I messed everything up already? "Sorry, Jacques," I said. "I should have asked before leaving. I just wanted to get out of the house for a bit."

"And *just* went to the market?" He eyed the trombone case in my hand. A detail Kesha and I had not prepared for.

"I stopped back at the Swamp. My old home. We'd forgotten it," I lied.

Jacques nodded. "I understand that, John. But we have rules in this house, and trust is very important. Most important. If you want to leave, you needn't ask for permission first. You just need to be honest with me."

I nodded, abashed. "I'm sorry, Jacques," I said again, while my dear clutched the basket tight.

Jacques stepped aside. "Miss Kesha, you may take the goods to the kitchen." He gestured for me to sit down on a bench just within the foyer entry. "My dear boy, there is a saying, 'Wildcats shall meet hyenas, goat-demons shall greet each other, there also Lilith shall, and find herself a resting place.' Do be careful where and with whom you rest. At any rate, I trust this is your father's instrument case?"

I bobbed my head in affirmation, having no clue about what the saying meant.

"I'm sorry to hear that it returned to your uncle's possession. That is very unfortunate for your father and his reputation, isn't it?"

"How's that?" I asked. Not knowing what Jacques knew.

"It took great effort for me to be assured it passed through the right hands from the time it was found to the time it was secured upon my request with Mama Loca."

"You know Mama Loca?" I swallowed hard.

"Is she not the aunt of Miss Kesha?" He looked at me with piercing eyes. "John, I know and have known everyone in this city."

"I'm sorry I lied."

"John, if I have not made you feel welcome and safe, it is I who should apologize for being less of a host than I aim." His eyes softened. "Can you ever forgive me?" His apology threw me. I couldn't tell if it was sincere. Something about His movements made me feel like prey being teased by a predator.

"Um, yes, but...I can't remember my evening. Any of my evenings. For months. The scene to which I awoke was...unsettling."

"Mmmm."

I felt the need to keep speaking my mind. "I...I can hear." I turned my head, showing the bad ear that once was. "I feel stronger. My brother. He...where is my brother?"

"At the risk of being a gossip, I believe he is upstairs in the company of Madam Arlington." Jacques gave a knowing grin. "I assure you, he is safe. It was she who came calling on him."

Kesha peeked around the corner.

I kept my attention focused on Jacques and nodded in understanding that my brother had also found someone to care for. There was so much more I wanted to ask. I couldn't.

"You should," He stated.

"Should what?"

"Ask."

"How do you know my thoughts?"

"My boy, I know things by my years. I know thoughts, or some of them, by your mannerisms of sorts. In truth, I know people. Most people don't know of me because they care not to ask. So, I implore you to ask."

"What happened last night? Well, what seemed like a night, but was many nights. I just don't know."

"You drank too much. Drink too much. But you appear to be enjoying the company. Does it not suit your appetite?"

"No." I reddened. "I mean, yes, I think so. It's...I had a feeling... visions really...pieces of the evening or evenings."

"The green fairy?"

"YES. YES. How? What?" Some relief poured over me. I wasn't losing my mind completely.

He patted my shoulder. Firm and understanding. "The drink."

"I...I saw a drink. I saw what you put..." I said cautiously. My next words did not form.

"Yes," he said. "Yes, you did. It was what you think," He said, not needing to hear more.

"I've read such a tale in my lessons. It can't be real."

Jacques laughed. "Bats, wolves, and the like? Do I seem like Vlad the Impaler? I don't even like horses, much less sweaty, angry men in metal suits. How droll."

I forced a laugh. I didn't have an answer. This conversation didn't seem to phase Him at all.

"Tell me, John." He turned, the stern look back on His face. His eyes flickered yellow, and He leaned in close.

I pulled away, but His hand still resting above my arm drew me in.

"How many of my guests lay in the comforts of my home...with their throats ripped out?"

"None that I've seen," I replied.

He nodded and opened his mouth wide.

I looked down at my shuffling feet.

He lifted my head gently with his finger under my chin.

"Look, John."

I raised my eyes to his teeth and then quickly down again.

"Not the mouth of a beast?"

"No, sir."

"Mhm." He released my chin and stroked His own, crossing His arms. "Then, Mr. John, aside from your inebriation, your keen sexual display that continues to rouse the fairest of this city, and your ample consumption of my food and drink." His voice raised, as did his temper. "Your pleasure-filled evenings drew fear from the pages of Stoker or the like? This is what you think of me and the gifts I have given you? And at what price to you? Healing? A full belly?" He waved His arms to show the expanse of the mansion. "A lavish dwelling of high beds and wanton servants to grant you any aid you may need?"

I had nothing left to accuse the man with. Still, my mouth and mind had not conferred. I blurted, "How can I hear my brother walk, and my feelings of faintness have all but gone since we met you?"

His stern face softened. "I see." He gave the question some thought before replying. "When does a scab on a wound fall?" He asked.

"When it heals?"

"And John, how does it heal?"

I shrugged.

"The composites within your body that grow and repair its host. The drink that I drink is offered to me by the finest in New Orleans. Rich bloodlines. Well-bred and married persons of power. They eat well. Embrace the sciences for their well-being. In exchange, I provide them...transactions. Introductions. Financing. Routes to their continued prosperity. Discreet sexual adventures. I gave you the same. From me. A pure bloodline. Healing. Of royal stock. You eat meat, do you not? Tasted milk from your mother's breast? Or from a goat? A cow? You feast upon the life of others no more. I give that to you as a gift. It is the ultimate gift of others, giving you their very life, is it not? You may ask then, why was I not fed blood in the Swamp?"

"I do not ask."

"Of course not. Because if you did, you would take from it disease such as consumption, syphilis, Spanish flu."

I nodded, feeling grateful for Jacques's patience and understanding. It lessened my shame and guilt. I was learning that life is different for those who have, versus those who have not. It was me in the wrong, I concluded.

The houseman, Terrance, approached, carrying a tray with two drinks.

"Thank you," I said, waving a hand. "I think I will pass. I'll try my hand at better moderation."

Jacques said nothing. His face wore disappointment as he took a goblet into his own hands and drank.

He sighed and licked the red liquid from His lips.

Upon consideration, I certainly didn't want to offend my host. "Well, maybe a small sip. Thank you."

Jacques smiled as I brought the drink to my lips. The smell and taste returned new memories to my mind. Had such hedonism actually occurred? Was I unfaithful to the one I adored? Had she known?

Jacques's eyes fell on my father's trombone case. "He was a delightful musician, your father. My life..." He again outstretched His arms, gesturing to the opulence of his wealth, "had become a bit of a bore. Within my soul, I felt nothing. I met your father some years ago." Jacques sighed as He reflected. "He had a gift for storytelling and emotion that came through that brass like no other I have ever heard."

I thought of the words Mama Loca had said of work to be done, and a home I had found. I was truly in a circle of my own paranoid thoughts and limited recollection.

"When your mother died, it was I who helped your father kill the man with whom your mother was unfaithful," Jacques confessed, without a tinge of emotion. "And then it stopped. He stopped."

My eyes widened. "But the murders continued, only stopping at his death."

Jacques nudged my hand, encouraging me to drink again.

I did as prodded, not wanting Him to stop his story. He was

telling me things about my family, things I'd never known or thought to put together.

"Indeed," He said. "The murders continued, though not by my hand. Certainly not by your father's."

"But the police believe it was him. And continued to investigate." Without planning to, I finished the drink, its taste and effects growing on my pallet and numbing my anxiety.

"So unfair. Such a blemish upon his legacy. Dear John, what do you think will happen to you, your brother, and your family name if discovered?"

"We'll have to leave New Orleans, our home. Even with the changing of our name. It wouldn't be enough."

"You are so wise. Your home is here if you choose and abide by house rules. What is it I can do for you? What do you think needs to be done to protect your family and your home?"

"Someone would need to kill another now that Father is gone. As the Axe Man. But I cannot kill an innocent man?"

"Is your concern only innocence?"

"Whomever I choose will have done nothing to me." A flicker of movement caught the corner of my eye. *Did I see the fairy again?*

"And what if they did something to your family?"

I shrugged, believing I would have the ability and drive. I jutted my chin and nodded. I tried in vain to be my brother and exhibit the courage he'd always possessed.

"This beast you thought I was, John. There are others in this city who are such men. Rippers who killed your mother. And then, despite such truths, mortal men seek to blame your father for the evil deeds of others. The reputation of your family has already been tarnished. Your parents were honest, hard-working people who only wanted to provide for their children. It pains me to think of the injustice."

"But...I thought."

His eyes yellowed. "You won't have to *think*. You only need to trust."

Jacques moved closer.

My head felt light.

Kesha peeked yet again from the corner. That same look of concern was written as a warning across her face.

The fairy appeared above me, rising higher. I tracked its flight around and around my head.

I felt a moment of that recurring pain before the pleasure followed, and then I returned to the abyss content in my paralysis in His arms.

CHAPTER II
COMPULSION

As I opened my eyes, fighting to recall the details of my conversation with Jacques just moments ago, I found myself standing in a courtyard, my hands and clothes soaked with blood. To my left stood Wayne. He was also bloodied and bewildered. He, however, was holding an axe. The axe from our father's trombone case.

Confused and disoriented, we gathered our whereabouts, trying to make sense of our surroundings in the early morning sun.

"John," he said, emotion building in his voice. "What did we do?"

I could feel my heart racing in my chest. I looked at Wayne, and he had the same look of confusion and fear on his face as I did. We both knew we had to figure out what had happened to us, and fast. Fragmented memories flooded my mind. Snapshots of a man and woman screaming, a small vision of us at night using a metal object to pry open a door before entering the unfamiliar home. Beyond that, there was nothing.

"Wayne," I said, "I have no recollection of how we got to this courtyard, or what happened to us. But I have a nightmarish vision of something horrible."

"A man...and a woman. Asleep in their bed," my brother said as he dropped the axe on the ground.

I nodded. "I receive visions of these pictures. Some vivid, some obscured. Moving pictures. Of faces. Acts. Like I'm watching myself from afar in a dream. Or on the wings of a fairy."

We pieced together our fragmented memories, trying to make sense of them. We remembered arguing with the man and woman, but we couldn't remember what it was about. We remembered using the screwdriver to pry open a door, but we didn't know whose door it was or what we were looking for.

The visions came in flashes, and we struggled to make sense of the nightmares we knew to be truths. Hazy, a memory returned. I sensed the terror and fear we must have caused them. I heard their pleas for help. Smelled the foul stench as we eviscerated their bodies.

We were alone, though we had each other. Baffled and scared, we felt consciously responsible for whatever happened, and the weight of it all was suffocating. We remained frozen in the courtyard, lost, trying to make sense of the horror show we seemed to have walked into—or caused.

I looked around for any clues. Our steps had stained the court-yard stones of Jacque's home. A path led to the high wall. It was there I spied the jars.

"Wayne." I pointed to the glass containers, dark in fill. "Look there."

He set off for a closer look.

A smear of our murder soilings ran the length of the enclosure to the top where the filled contents sat. I knew what must be inside.

"We filled them," he said. "I remember filling them from their bellies and arms and legs...and throat." My brother shuddered. Tears welled in his eyes, and he looked down at his hands as if he didn't recognize them. "What's happening to us?"

The answers were not there.

"Boys," a voice heralded.

Wayne and I turned to find Jacques standing at our heels, and we jumped back at the sight of him.

It was Kesha I spotted next, and Terrance following her close behind. He was carrying two buckets of water. She had her arms full of clean clothes.

"John, Wayne. Quick."

Before I could utter a word, hot water doused my body. I felt the droplets splash me as my brother received his cleansing. The houseman raced back inside, empty buckets in tow.

Kesha tugged at our bloodied garments, paying them no heed and saying nothing more until they were gathered in a heap, outpouring shades of red and pink that flowed to the sewer drain.

The houseman returned with another onslaught of hot water.

I heard a muffled thump and turned to find Jacques behind us, his arms full of the vessels from the wall cap. "Surely, you must be famished," he stated as we remained in want for answers, naked in the open courtyard being scrubbed and wiped and not caring at all.

Are we in Hell? Are we truly still in the world we once knew, or have we traveled to another life, where lucidity does not exist?

To my surprise, Wayne advanced to Jacques, his arm outstretched. "I'd like a drink."

My eyes fell to Kesha's, which were staring back into my own. She shook her head to me and pulled a clean shirt over my damp head.

"Wayne, perhaps we—" I began, but the jar was to his lips already.

He drank until he coughed.

Turning to me, it was tears, not water droplets, tumbling down his cheeks. "Help me," he begged. "I can't stop."

"I'll find a way," I promised him. Promised myself.

Jacques seemed amused.

Kesha leaned in to my ear and whispered something.

I nodded, thinking I loved her but struggling to find any intimate moments and conversations stored in my head. I searched for a feeling, an instinct. A trust.

She brushed her hand along mine before gathering the wet, bloodied heap.

At her touch, the thump of her heart through her hand invigorated my spirit.

Jacques stared at her, his dark brow dropped in disapproval. He reached for Wayne's jar and took it for himself, consuming it until it was empty. Then he dashed the glass against the wall before stomping back indoors as the morning light rose higher and heat of the day followed.

We still lacked answers.

The axe lay alone, knowing the truth.

I stood alone, with the same veracity.

CHAPTER 12
LIGHT

I t was shared with me how Eddie the Glove made it a point to pass by each beat cop corner on his early morning walk. He'd never ask what mayhem may have befallen the Quarter while he slept, but the policemen shared freely as if Eddie were their priest. He'd done this for years, even before the Axe Man started his killing spree. Eddie was the one who'd come up with the murderer's nickname.

He heard it from one policeman during his morning walks. The police believed the Axe Man had committed at least six murders and several attacks in the past year. The attacks were brutal and unprovoked, and the police had no leads on the killer.

"He's at it again," the cop said by way of greeting Eddie.

"Morning. Maybe you can start me off right ways. I don't have the foggiest of what you say."

"Axe Man," the policeman clarified. "I thought maybe we'd seen the last. Most thought it was that old trombonist on a vendetta for his wayward wife."

"Hmm." Eddie stretched his back, nodding to passersby. "Grocer?"

The cop nodded. "Yep. And Italian. Steve Boca. He got away with a knock on the head. Can't recall a thing. The other couple didn't fare so well."

"Other couple, you say?"

"Just next door."

Eddie squinted, deep in thought.

"Boca made it to Frank Genusa's before he collapsed. Axe Man must not have been done for the night. That or he thought Boca went to the other house."

"Tells me the killer may not have given chase. Strange."

The policeman shrugged in indifference. "He must have been pretty mad about it. Chopped 'em up good. Chief wants to keep the investigation clean. Keeping Boca and the couple different. Doesn't want to cause a panic. If they say Axe Man is only after Dego grocers, it means everyone else is safe."

Eddie chuckled, not in humor, but in disbelief. "Grocers. There's still no motive for the murders. The victims were chosen at random. No obvious pattern. Trudeau Lecartier could have been good for one murder if, in fact, his wife was having a discreet encounter, but quite unlikely, given the family. Has anyone spoken to his boys since the passing?"

"In the Swamp? Can't say anyone is too fixed on finding anyone in there."

"Hmm." Eddied nodded, patting the officer on the shoulder.

"Forget something back at home?" the officer called out as Eddie turned back in the direction he'd come from.

"Think I'll head over to the Swamp," said Eddie, his hand sliding to his rear pocket, finding gloves within his grasp.

"Don't suppose I can convince you not to," the officer called. "We're not going in there to get you."

Eddie waved a hand as he ventured toward the danger.

As he strolled to the darker part of town at the water's edge, he thought about several clues investigators could gather from the crime scenes. In each case, the killer had gained access to the victims' homes by chiseling a hole in the back door or prying a way in. The killer then made his way to the victims' bedrooms and attacked them while they slept. In the past year of killings, investigators also found several bloody footprints at the crime scenes, leading them to believe the killer had entered the homes barefoot.

The key returned to motive. The Quarters had its share of violent deaths. They were often individual vendettas, gang and turf violence rooted in underground criminal activities, or general street segregation. The reason for the Axe Man's targeting of Italian grocers was not entirely clear, but Eddie speculated a perceived slight or some other reason. Others had suggested the grocers may have been targeted because they were easy victims, given that they often carried sizable sums of cash in their stores, but sometimes money, valuable heirlooms, and other items of potential value were left behind.

It wasn't long after passing Jackson Square that he entered the dangerous streets of New Orleans' French Quarter neighborhood, known as the Swamp. As a well-dressed African-American man, the locals would pay him no mind, short of lesser hoodlums and visiting degenerates. Soon, he could feel the suspicious glares of such onlookers upon him. The street was seedy, and the early morning drunks leaving the houses of ill repute only added to the menacing atmosphere. The still intoxicated men stumbled around in the early morning from the opium den or their desperate mistresses. It seemed to be the norm there of unspeakable deeds dwelling in dark shadows.

Eddie had a feeling that morning would be different. He had a hunch he would find something that would lead him closer to the Axe Man. He walked down the alleyway, careful not to make any sudden movements. Suddenly, he felt someone grab him from behind. He struggled to break free, but the attacker was too strong. He pressed a cold metal object to Eddie's temple.

His senses, keen and raised, alerted Eddie to four aggressive-looking men wielding big wooden sticks before him. They were quick to form a human barricade blocking his path.

"Lost your way, old man?"

"Looking for the sons of Trudeau Lecartier."

"Won't find them here. Probably as dead as their old man. You'd best head back to Tremé or the Seventh Ward. Wherever you've come from. We ain't your people."

Eyeing their pulsing jugulars, the men's hearts raced, readying for conflict.

Eddie, too, braced himself for the inevitable fight.

The men approached him.

Eddie knew when he set foot into the Swamp he was not welcome, but this was where answers would be found. He would not back down.

One of the Live Oak Boys readied for a swing.

Eddie snatched from his back pocket the heavy sand-filled glove, ready to use it to defend himself. The men attacked him with their sticks, but Eddie expertly dodged their attempts, fighting back with his namesake whizzing through the air, finding its mark with crushing blows.

After a few minutes of fierce fighting, the attackers lay in a semicircle, beaten and bloodied.

"Who in this neighborhood knows their whereabouts?"

"Bugger off."

Eddie didn't say a word. He simply stepped forward, bent, and grabbed the man by the throat, squeezing until he could feel the man's windpipe constricting.

"Where is he?" Eddie growled, his eyes yellowing, boring into the man's.

The man struggled to speak, his face red as he gasped for air, but Eddie didn't let go. He squeezed harder until the man's eyes bulged and he went limp.

Eddie released the man and turned to the others.

"Who's next?" he said, his voice steady.

The men hesitated, unsure of what to do. Eddie didn't wait for them to make a move. He lunged forward with wildcat speed and grabbed another man by the arm, twisting until he heard the bone snap.

"Where is he?" Eddie demanded, his face twisting with rage. "Enough playing around."

The man screamed in pain, but Eddie didn't let up. He twisted harder until the man was writhing on the ground in agony, his bone popping through his skin.

It went on like that for a minute. Eddie brutalized the men, breaking their fingers, arms, stepping on their necks, and doing whatever he had to do to get the information he needed.

Finally, one man cracked. He told Eddie everything he wanted to know. Eddie left the gang members there, bleeding and broken, as he went off in pursuit of his target.

The streets were empty; the rain started coming down in sheets. But Eddie didn't care. He had what he needed. And he knew he would do it all again if he had to. Because that was what he did. He was Eddie the Glove, and he always got what he wanted. No matter the cost.

Despite the danger that lay ahead, the man strode confidently towards Uncle John's club, determined to find the Carter brothers and end their nefarious activities. He knew he was risking exposure, but he was willing to do whatever it took to bring justice to this dangerous city.

Eddie stepped into the Fireproof Saloon, the stench of sweat, sex, and spilled booze assaulting his nostrils. The jazz band played on, horns blaring a raucous tune that echoed off the walls. Rough men huddled in corners, drinking cheap whiskey and gin. They lustfully eyed the prostitutes who roamed the room. Sailors, drunks, and lost souls all mingled together, looking for a momentary escape from the harsh realities of life. The whores, scarred on the inside and out, with no escape from theirs.

Eddie tried to blend in; his dark skin helped in the dimly lit room. He crossed the room to the bar, keeping a benign profile, but the men's eyes left the women and traced Eddie's every step. The bartender gave him a cautious nod of warning, but Eddie ignored it. He had a job to do.

"Whiskey," he said, his voice low and steady. Monies placed on the bar, following the ask.

The bartender poured him a glass, and Eddie swallowed it whole, the burn of the alcohol sliding down his throat. He knew he had to be careful here. The wrong move could get him killed.

"Another." He pushed the glass forward and reached into his pocket to cover the tab.

"Last one," the bartender replied, giving Eddie a generous pour.

"Maybe," Eddie said. "I'll leave right after a word with the owner, John Swan."

The bartender grimaced. "He's in a foul mood today, Eddie."

"Yeah, so am I." Eddie swallowed the second glass and slammed it down. "I'll have one more while you fetch him."

The bartender filled the short glass and disappeared into the back room. Eddie waited, his eyes scanning his surroundings for any sign of trouble. He met the eyes of the musicians on stage, who gave him a wink or nod as they played.

A few minutes later, John Swan emerged from a back room, his massive frame towering over Eddie. He rolled up his sleeves, and Eddie tensed, ready for a fight.

"I'm here as a patron. Not the law."

"Your patronage is not welcome." John slapped his massive hand over the coins and slid them toward Eddie but off the table. "Don't want your money, neither."

"Are the boys staying with Jacques?" Eddie asked, trying to keep his voice calm.

John didn't want to cooperate, but Eddie could see the surprise in the big Irishman's eyes. He knew he was on to something.

John toyed with his mouth, his jaw jutting about in contemplation.

The men Eddie had interrogated earlier, the Live Oak Boys gang, stumbled into the saloon carrying one another, beaten, broken, and bruised. They pointed to Eddie, and John's expression hardened.

"I'll let you leave if you tell me the killings last night weren't by the Axe Man," John said, his voice low and menacing. "We all know the actual killer was Trudeau Lecartier, God damn his soul for the death he's brought to this city."

Eddie hesitated, his mind racing. He knew about the killings, but he didn't have any evidence yet. But he had to take the chance.

"Yes," he said, his voice low. "There were killings. But a grocer escaped. Same pattern. Same feel."

John nodded, unsatisfied. "Get out of here, and make sure your boys do their jobs," he said, his eyes following Eddie as he made his way to the door. "Trudeau Lecartier is still your man," he shouted in frustration, then slapped the glass from the bar to the ground. As it shattered, John trudged away and back upstairs.

Eddie left the Fireproof Saloon, his heart pulsing with adrenaline. He knew he was getting closer to the truth. But he also knew the danger for the boys was just beginning.

CHAPTER 13
DENOUNCE

It was a time and place Kesha had whispered to me in the courtyard. I found myself with great caution that Jacques not be privy to this information, despite his overtures of freedom and trust. I was eager to oblige her request with interest in both the woman who enchanted me and answers she may provide.

She was waiting by the entryway door. With a wide-brimmed hat, long-sleeved dress, and ivory lace parasol umbrella in hand, she looked to be of elite social class. I was breathless.

Kesha saw as much in my expression and smiled before hiding it with her hand. She muttered, "Your new clothes suit you."

"You are too precious," I said, reaching discretely for her hand. "In all my cursed nightmares of late, it is you I search for in dreams."

She lowered her eyes. "I've rarely had a man speak to me and look at me the way you do, John Carter. Let's go where it is safe to speak our hearts."

"Where should we go?" I asked, envisioning a lovely park or a stroll along the waterway.

"Lafayette."

"The cemetery?" Any notions of romance vanished, and my dark thoughts returned. Before we left the mansion, I looked up the majestic staircase to my brother's chambers. The door was closed. He'd been understandably quiet of late. More distant than I'd ever known. I missed my brother and the modest but free life we'd once had.

I reached for the door handle and felt her hand on my shoulder. As I opened the door and Kesha passed, the hand remained. It squeezed.

"More secrets?" Jacques asked.

I turned to face a grin I was learning was more menacing than of genuine humor.

"No secrets, Jacques," I replied. My voice trembled. "We're stepping out for a stroll, if you care to join us?"

"And steal the time you have for love? Tsk, tsk." He shook his finger. "My fellow Frenchmen would further disown me should I step in the way of a budding romance. That is what you intend to pursue, is it not? With my...hired help?"

Unease grew in my stomach. Perhaps it was how he posed as understanding while wearing a veil of dissatisfaction. He spun his words like a web, trapping anyone stupid enough to engage with him. I questioned whether I should leave, and whether I was putting Kesha in harm's way.

Kesha spoke. "Monsieur Jacques, we won't be long. I think Mr. John could use some fresh air to clear his head and be of the right mind, should you require his services this eve. My tasks for the time being are complete."

"Very well." Jacques turned on his heels and waved from behind. "It will allow me more time with your brother, John."

The door slammed before I could think. Kesha tugged my arm to leave.

I was torn.

As Kesha and I walked hand in hand through the labyrinthine paths of the New Orleans cemetery, I was present in form, but not in mind. Visions of terror flashed before my eyes. Leaving Wayne again tugged at my conscience. The weight of life's decisions and mortality pressed down on me with an unbearable strain, thinking of all I had to endure just to thrive or survive, seemingly at the expense of others' lives.

The atmosphere was thick with the scent of flowers and sound of mourning doves, but I couldn't shake off the feeling that we were walking in the land of the dead, which further compounded my despair.

The grand above-ground vaults loomed above us, casting eerie shadows on the ground. The silence of our somber stroll was broken only by the distant sound of a rousing musician playing a trumpet and rustle of the remaining fall leaves blowing under our feet.

Kesha's voice broke the silence. "What are you thinking about, John?"

"Forgive me. I'm thinking how thoughts of you have been replaced here in our surroundings, and I am consumed by the riddles of the world I now know to be true," I replied. Her silence coaxed me to keep going. "About how uncertain my life has been and how death may be the only certainty we have for escape. I fear it is closer to me than it has ever been before. All starting with our host, your employer, Mr. Jacques. I believe that my brother and I are making a grave error by staying, and yet, I cannot imagine not seeing you. I also can't imagine returning to the life Wayne and I once knew. Why is it you must stay?"

Kesha squeezed my hand gently. "It takes someone strong to survive the brutality of our lives, but it takes someone near beyond human to endure an eternity of living. Death for someone undead may actually be a mercy. Life may be a damnation for some people. I stay because I have nearly nothing left, family long gone. For now, it is my burden to live in service to Jacques, at the request of my aunt in the Quarters. I bear the weight of what Jacques demands of me, too, as it was he who brought us to New Orleans. Living under his roof gives me protection in the Quarters."

Her words made me shiver. The idea of this eternal life, being trapped in this world or the next, was daunting. But the thought of death being the only release from a life of struggle and poverty made me question everything I had ever believed in. The price for wealth under Jacques would be killing others but us living on. The cost for betrayal was certain death and a brief life of misery and hopelessness, unless I could live and recreate such a life with Kesha. But what could I provide us? A life on the streets? I had nothing. I was no one.

My eyes read every engraved name we passed. We were mere yards from my own parents' entombment. I said, "My family struggled to make ends meet. We were poor to a level they could never escape. Now I wonder if their death was actually freedom. For my father, I believe it was. My mother died with secrets. Secrets that came from possibly her pursuit of a better or easier life."

Kesha nodded, understanding my pain. She paused in front of a grand vault, her hand tracing the intricate carvings on its surface. "I feel the enduring heaviness of having to live in a house of horrors, but to protect my family gives me a purpose."

"What purpose is mine other than want or greed? My brother and I considered making our own fortunes, starting with Mr. Jacques. We made a grievous error trying to take what was not ours, and then embraced the opportunity to earn it after the foiling of our plot. It appears our 'work' is a payment to him in debauchery, devilishness, and murder. I cannot fathom how you can pity me, much less choose to be in my very presence with certain damnation."

Kesha squeezed my hand. "You still have the freedom to make your own path, to find your true purpose. Choices that will last a lifetime. I would hope to be part of that. I never expected you to be who you are."

I looked at her and wondered how someone so young could possess such wisdom.

"I think I've found someone who is worth living a life of uncertainty with, knowing they are pure of heart, caring, and worth sacrifice," I said, looking into Kesha's eyes.

"It's only now, after meeting you, that I question that purpose," she continued. "Maybe I've found someone worth a sacrifice of my own."

I felt a warmth spread through my chest as I realized what she was saying.

We continued walking through the cemetery, lost in our own thoughts. The surrounding atmosphere seemed to shift, the shadows growing longer and silence more profound. But with Kesha by my side, I felt like I could face anything. The uncertainty of life no longer felt like Hell itself, but a challenge I would undertake for her. As we continued to walk, hand in hand, I felt a glimmer of hope that maybe, just maybe, life wasn't the damnation I believed it to be. Maybe, with Kesha in my life and Wayne having our backs, we could find some sort of happiness, even in the uncertainty of our mortality and life under Jacques's roof. These things, I would have to share with my brother. He seemed a lot more lost, with no one to pull him back. I had to be that someone.

As we walked out of the cemetery, I couldn't help feeling a sense of security. The glimmer was no longer just a distant light, but a flame that burned brightly in my heart.

At the time, I was unaware that Wayne was being seduced by

another while I was falling under my own delusions of hope and being pulled further from my flesh and blood.

Far from our footsteps and keeping distance, someone followed.

CHAPTER 14
CHANNELING

Wayne lay in his bedchamber, contemplating the confusing courtyard events, while we were away. He shared later that he was hoping to speak with Jacques, when there was a light rap on the door.

"Enter," he welcomed and sat upright to greet the one he'd hoped would beckon.

"Do you sleep?" Jacques asked, carrying an armful of fine clothing and small box. "I can come back another time. You've had quite...the evening."

"Indeed." Wayne's voice was flat. He spun around on the bed, his legs dangling to the floor. "Jacques, if I may ask, exactly who are you, and what are your intentions with us?" The mysterious man stopped, smiled knowingly at the boy, and diverted his attention to the items in his hands.

"I come bearing gifts. I took the liberty of purchasing some more suitable attire for your rising stature. Compliments of Royal's very finest tailors, Herriman & Chesse. And for your loyalty," Jacques opened the small box, "I present to you a suitable timepiece."

Wayne admired the watch with heartfelt appreciation. "Thank you, Jacques. This is more than I could have asked. I would never think to ask." The words came out as a whimper.

"Which is what makes giving and receiving gifts even more pleasurable for both parties," Jacques stated, attempting to ease Wayne's spirits.

"I'm sorry to burden you with any doubt. This level of hospitality just seems beyond our own worth."

"You boys are never short of questions or self-doubt. Although in you, I sense something quite different from your brother. Confidence and strength, I can help you develop. And I can't help noticing how your brother appears to douse that wonderful spirit of yours."

"John and I are a good team. He thinking for the future, I for the moment."

"And what do you seek in *this* moment? What can you see of your own destiny when you have someone able to help you kindle it to the brightness you desire?" Jacques asked, walking toward the window and drawing the curtains tight. The light vanished, save for what came through the doorway. Wayne gathered some of that courage Jacques was complimenting just a moment ago and spoke his mind.

"I want to know, why do we no longer have our thoughts and memories? Why are your chores for us wiped from our own minds? I assure you, you don't need to spare me of my own deeds. I am up for any task."

"Then you shall be granted your thoughts. Some, in due time. Tonight, you will fill yet more jars. Remove another wretch from this city that they sin no more. And I shall pay handsomely to further reward your efforts and trust."

"Is that what happened last night? We murdered someone... some people...less than innocent?"

"None of us are innocent, Mr. Wayne." Jacques sat on the bed aside from him, putting his arm around the young man. "You have the makings of a warrior. A killer commits acts of selfishness. You are waging war with evil. I have seen the determination in your eyes. This you proved the moment you leveled a weapon at me and fired."

"I was a killer in that instant, fighting for no one but my brother and myself. I watched the bullets hit their mark. How is it...that... well, how are you-"

"You hit me, my dear boy. I saw death in your eyes. The mind of a Spartan born before me. How lucky I was to witness its birth."

Wayne swallowed hard. Jacques didn't seem afraid or mad. He looked at Wayne like some sort of champion and excitedly drew him closer.

"I just want to earn a place," Wayne confessed. "To have a place. To know comforts and not pain or uncertainty."

"Life is painful and uncertain. Death is pain and uncertainty. We live with this for our tomorrows." Jacques moved his head toward Wayne's ear. "You must embrace the pain to see through it to the pleasure."

Wayne slipped from Jacques's encroachment and stood. "Are you dead?" he asked resolutely.

"Am I not here before you?" Jacques got up, his shadow trapping Wayne in a prison of intimidation. His smile became threatening, edging closer in a game of pursuit.

"I know of stories of the undead. Fables of the French Quarter. Night stalkers who know no death and take their victims for blood."

"Do you wish to accuse me?" Jacques reached for Wayne's arm. "Or join me?"

Wayne stepped closer to the window's heavy drapes. "How is it you walk in the day?"

"One foot in front of the other, like all men." Jacques moved again toward Wayne. "Like so."

"That's not what I mean. Enough of the riddles." Wayne side-stepped away. "Tell me the truths, so I can know them and decide."

"YOU? Decide?" Jacques rushed in and shoved Wayne across the room, sending him over a sitting chair and into the wall. Hanging pictures fell and shattered. Jacques advanced.

"I JUST NEED TO KNOW!" Wayne shouted, recovering quickly to his feet.

Jacques paid no heed. He lifted a large shard of glass from the floor and ran it across his own arm. The blood flowed freely. "I am a disease. A man of sciences and alchemist in a former profession. The tales you speak of...night walkers. They prefer to do so from a sickness of the body, porphyria. Itching, rashing, burning from the sun." Jacques gripped the drapes, running them through his fingers. "Our gums recede. Our teeth, therefore, appear longer. The light can damage our skin, so our noses and ears may fall off. The madness from rabies flows through our blood. It takes our humanity. We take the blood of others, not just for strength, but for purification. For a cure. We inherit a burden with a bounty of priceless gifts."

"And this was put upon you by another?" Wayne asked quietly.

"It is the price we pay for the lifestyle of the elite. Apex predator. To drink another human's blood, to dine on their flesh. To shake the hand of the devil himself, gazing into his eyes, and embracing him as a friend." Jacques offered his bleeding arm to Wayne. "Take. Take from me. When you receive from the highest stock in human nature, you take from their essence. Their strengths. Were you and your brother not lame? Afflicted? Do you think it was the devil's work or sorcery that healed you? Look him in the eye, my boy. Welcome the long-lost friend."

Wayne drew closer; he could barely hear Jacques's words. They began to swim and thump with his heartbeat. He took Jacques's arm in his hand, the blood dripping to the floor.

"I do not make you a monster. I unleash from you what is already inside. I give you the strength of my bloodline. The richness of all I have to give. But to receive, you must take. And taking is in your nature, my dear...savage boy.

Wayne placed his lips on Jacques's arm and suckled with greed.

"Take your place among the true vampires of this city, and I shall give you the riches you deserve, the confidence you seek, and the family you long for...before your brother leaves you, too."

"I want it," he said. "I want it all."

CHAPTER 15
CONTROL

Kesha and I returned to Jacques with renewed spirit and resolve. Kesha bid me goodbye, as she had her own work to attend to.

The clinking of tea cups came from the parlor, so I stepped inside for a casual look, hoping my presence would not be inappropriate should any of Jacques's business associates or high society friends be in private conversation.

My new outlook faded as I saw my brother and Jacques waiting for me. Immediately, I could tell something was off. The air sent warning prickles up the back of my neck.

"Ah, at last, I can see my brother," Wayne said, greeting me with a strained smile and gesturing for me to take a seat. He wore a fine watch of golden metal and rich leather banding, no doubt a gift from our host. Jacques sat quietly, observing me with his dark eyes. His legs were crossed, and upon them rested his teacup in hand. He lifted it and took a loud, drawn-out slurp.

"We need to talk, John," Wayne said, his voice serious.

"Of course." I sat on the edge of a large leather armchair, my elbows straining to reach either side. I swallowed hard, wondering what this could be about. My mind raced with possibilities, but nothing prepared me for what they shared next.

"As a genuine test of our abilities and commitment to our employer and host, Jacques and I have decided to complete a task tonight," Wayne said, his voice low. "We will call upon a man of Jacques's choosing, our memory and decisions our own."

My heart sank at his words. I couldn't believe what I was hearing. Another murder? I felt sick.

I tried to appeal to their sense of reason, urging them to reconsider, but my brother remained steadfast, his eyes hard and unyielding.

"John, it serves a purpose. Jacques assures me the man is...less than honorable, involved in crimes against our city and its citizens. It will be a service to Jacques and the Quarter. A service to our father." I watched my brother with horror. He believed every word that came out of his mouth.

Jacques remained silent, watching us both with an inscrutable expression.

Wayne turned to Jacques. "Please, tell us what you have learned from your inquiries."

"It would be my pleasure." Jacques placed the cup and saucer at his side and leaned back in his chair. Though the furniture was large and overstuffed, our host never looked small. He appeared to command the seat like a rider upon a horse. Everything about him exuded confidence and strength. "Boys, this task is actually to your benefit. I, too, had to commit an unthinkable act for your protection as a ruse of another grocer attack. A sacrifice I will endure—for your benefit. It is true that your mother did not act with discretion or honor to your father or family. Your father discovered who the man was, and he was most justifiably dispatched. Not being a man of violence, your father went to your uncle for counsel. It was then that things took a turn. I'm afraid, while your father fell into deep regret and guilt for his deed, your uncle seized the opportunity to continue murdering men and women who had expanded Italian criminal influence with storefronts in the Quarter, a task he seconded to his cronies and business partner Joseph Mumfre. His rationale, fear, and power would drive the Italians out of the neighborhood in a property grab scheme, so your uncle could expand his businesses beyond the establishments of ill repute in Storyville. He attempted to lay blame on your father upon his death." Jacques sat back. His expression was one of distaste, having been the bearer of bad news to his own suffering.

I listened, fully fixed by the story so far-fetched, it had been erased from my family connection. It seemed preposterous but perfectly plausible. Logic I was willing to accept, for it was Jacques delivering the truths.

"Your father's death and the murders stopping prompted investigators to close the case of these unprovoked killings. The murder you committed last night pushed them to question their suspect and motive. One that has vexed authorities and most certainly your uncle."

Wayne added, "This is why uncle inquired about Father's instrument case. He'd stored the axe within for authorities to discover."

I took a deep breath, taking in all of the life I had felt was long left behind. I was conflicted. On the one hand, I didn't want to be a part of this murder. I didn't care about any of this. It just felt like burying shit under more shit. But I could see how lost in it Wayne already was. There was a touch of crazy in his eyes identical to that in Jacques's. Could I abandon my brother? On the other hand, I didn't want to leave. I wanted to stay in this house. Stay with Kesha. She was my light in all of this, the one thing that made living worth it. As the tension in the room grew, I knew I had to make a choice. It was leave the house with Kesha...if she would follow...and escape this madness, or stay and be a part of something I knew was wrong. As I looked at my brother and Jacques, I knew this was not a decision I could make lightly. Their expectations were clear, and the consequences of my decision would be dire.

Finally, I spoke, trying to flip the argument and buy more time to think. "If the men we are to kill are evil in their own right and deserve to be punished, I urge you to rethink. Perhaps in the end, it is Uncle who should be led to the slaughter. For then, the mystery of the Axe Man can remain. He shall atone for these crimes, and our own links can be forever be removed now that we are the Carters. Members of a different ilk? Men of their own makings."

Wayne jumped from his chair and embraced me. "I knew you would agree."

"Then it is settled." Jacques clapped. "For a moment, I thought you would decline and we'd have another matter to tend to. Although, men of your own makings, I might challenge." Jacques glared at me with hard eyes. His face expressionless.

I questioned which would be my greatest sacrifice, my love, my survival, or my character. In my quest to find strength and freedom, I was growing weaker and lacked the ability to challenge the monster who might altogether defeat me. Surely, if tonight I could kill a man, my family, my uncle–despite how much I despised him–then I could bring myself to kill Jacques. By what means, I hadn't a clue. I had met the devil and knew him not to be a friend.

CHAPTER 16
HELP

Our uncle had been little in our lives. Still, we knew him well, and knew of his habits, and that he footed our bills. He frequented the establishments he owned in the early evening, making his presence known to give anyone a second thought about fleecing his business or battering his prostitutes. He would make the rounds again, this time with many whiskies under his belt to collect the night's earnings and dole out wages. He had a mistress he would call on well after the clubs and brothels closed, and he would be back out before daylight, so he could sleep in the warmth of his betrothed before breakfast.

We departed Jacques's after the clock chimed thrice, waiting in the shadows of our old haunt, the Swamp. Sights, sounds, and smells had not changed in the last few months, but the assault on my senses and that of Wayne's reminded us that this was not a place we wished to return to.

It was I who spotted our uncle first. He seemed bigger than I recalled, and I'd forgotten the large stick he carried like that of his old crew.

As Wayne and I stalked our uncle down the seedy streets with just a sliver of moonlight casting a light glow on the decrepit neighborhood, I couldn't help feeling the recurring pit in my gut and grip tightening in my chest. I questioned the murder we were about to commit, but Wayne had no misgivings and insisted we must see it through.

My insecurity persisted. "Are you sure about this, Wayne?" I asked, my voice barely above a whisper.

"Positive," he replied, his tone resolute. "We can't let him get away with what he's done to us. And it's what Jacques asked of us. We agreed. If you turn away now, you turn from me." Wayne reached into his pocket. "I was going to give you your half later." My brother stuffed a handful of paper bills into mine. "It's more than Father and Mother earned in a year."

"Jacques now paying us beyond our stay and meals?"

"And everything else he's giving us. He told me he can even make gold from other metals. He's a man of science." Wayne turned to me, looking deep into my eyes. "We're going to be rich, John, but you have to do *your* part, and that means forgetting about your servant girl. Jacques warned me that while she works for her keep and does a fine job about the house, she's linked to witches and should not be trusted."

"She's no witch." My heart had now doubled its pounding in my chest.

"Let's just say Jacques questions your loyalty and priorities. Don't make me doubt you, too. Now come on, Uncle's about to turn off at the corner."

"Fine," I relented. This was the only way to get what I wanted.

Stay with my brother.

Stay with Kesha.

Murder Uncle.

"And you have the pistol?" I asked.

"Jacques said you had it." My brother froze, realizing we had embarked upon a murder without a weapon.

"He told me you would do it," I deflected. "That you'd already spoken of it."

With Wayne focused on our pursuit and my mind swirling in my head, neither of us had thought to look behind us. In a flurry of thumps and cracks, four of our uncle's fellow gang members came up from our rear and attacked. We fell to the ground, dazed from the sudden blows, the wind knocked out of us. The bludgeoning continued against our legs, arms, and skulls. I pulled myself into a ball, hoping to absorb some of the blows.

Through watered and swelling eyes, I could see the blur of Uncle approaching us. I couldn't see his eyes, but I knew they were cold and cruel. He, too, joined in the thrashing, and I could feel myself slipping away into unconsciousness as he cursed us.

"You boys are causing me problems. Visits I should not have as a respectable businessman." He kicked my brother's ribs.

But then, something strange happened. A dark, silhouetted figure appeared out of nowhere, attacking our uncle and his men with a ferocity that was otherworldly. The men and our uncle screamed as their bodies were decimated by this unknown demon of the night. I continued to slip into darkness as their screams echoed in my ears. Right before I disappeared, I heard a voice, but this time it was not Jacques.

When I awoke, I was lying in a small bed. Wayne was next to me, his face bruised and battered. We looked at each other in silence, both of us knowing something strange and inexplicable had happened that night, and now, we were not in the home of Jacques.

A man I did not know sat rocking on a thin railed chair, in the corner of the small room. He smoked a cigarette and held a glass goblet. Bourbon was my guess.

"There you come," he said, taking a drag and flicking ash on his own floor.

He was a colored man. Maybe sixty, judging by his grey and white hair wrapped around his balding head. He had mutton chops, and his eyes were yellow, as if jaundiced. They bulged from the thin pink skin of his eyelids that were exposed and unfolded.

"I can give you a glass if you need something for the pain. Bit early for breakfast, but I can put on a pot of grits if you need warmth to soothe your bruised bellies."

"We're fine," Wayne replied, his voice as bruised as our bodies. "We need to go."

"Mmm." The man swallowed the rest of his drink, which was substantial, and rose to his feet. "Looks to me by your lack of fighting skills or strength that you've not turned."

My eyes widened. "Turned?" I asked, now fully attentive.

"You stay at Jacques, right?" He poured another four fingers of amber booze from an unbranded bottle. "I'm only asking so I can help you."

"I know who you are," Wayne said.

I still could not place the face.

"And I know who you are. That could make us fast friends, or it could complicate things."

"How do you know us?" I asked.

"You're Trudeau's boys. I enjoyed your father's gift. Watched him play with all of our city's best. He remains missed. You all have been missing, too. So, I'll ask again. Stayin' with Jacques?"

"Everyone loved our father. They just never paid him to show that love. You know the answer to your question, Detective." Wayne stood from the bed, with a grunt. "We need to go, John. Now."

"I'm no threat, boys. I don't care what you did to your uncle...or rather, tried to do. Trust me. I'd had a mind to do it myself before last night. Don't really care about why you left your home either. Seems pretty clear to me. Same story as most of us in this city. What I do care about is more murders in the Quarter just so you can fill an unending appetite if you stay in that place you're staying. I want you to know you can do the right thing by telling me. What Jacques is doing to you is not your fault. There is a way out."

"You know nothing of Jacques. You know nothing of us. My father meant nothing, so you mean nothing." Wayne grabbed my shirt, pulling me toward the door. I felt so out of place, unable to ask the right questions or connect the dots.

"He'll make you promises. He'll have you do things you know you shouldn't do. He'll damn you. Promise you life after death," the man shouted after us, and Wayne slowed down. "The streets are tough these days without drawing attention. You won't get turned if there isn't enough food supply. Won't even turn the rich, who have much more to offer. You either have to be special these days or be among the victims who are turned by the reckless. The rippers."

Wayne put his hand to the door but hesitated. I glanced at him, my heart beating in my ears. Wayne turned. "How do you know this?"

I, too, was beyond curious and not quite following all that was being conveyed. It appeared my brother had the benefit of more information than I did.

"Some of them got to me, too. There are Others. The ones who killed your mother. Let me tell you what you can do to save yourselves. How to get out of that house of lies."

CHAPTER 17

THREAT

ayne and I received more than an earful from Eddie. It was enough to spur on that seed of doubt that was already there. Deep panic set in when we left him, a man who seemed to have our best interests at heart. We had no choice but to return to Jacques, a place where my brother and I were in an endless cycle of tension.

We barely spoke on the way; our heads hung low in defeat and expectation of our host and employer's anger and disappointment. We felt it as soon as we stepped through the door. Indeed, my brother Wayne and I had utterly failed our first conscious assignment.

Jacques was pacing back and forth in the dimly lit living room when we arrived.He ignored us as we walked in, which made me even more nervous. Jacques's tall, imposing figure stood in the corner, his back to us. Wayne and I stood sweating in our suits, waiting for him to speak. Wishing he wouldn't speak. His compelling voice made you want to do what he said. Yearn for it deep in your bones. I shuddered at that voice.

Wayne fidgeted with his new watch.

"Sit down," Jacques said at long last, gesturing to the couch. We did as we were told, both of us too scared to speak.

He stood in front of us, his arms crossed over his chest. Even in our childhood, I could not recall a household of such discipline. Part of me welcomed it. Part of me loathed it. I struggled to understand if it was care or disdain we were receiving. My head on the matter swayed like a pendulum every day.

"What happened?" he demanded, his eyes piercing our souls. "I gave you a job to do, and you failed. You know what that means, don't you?"

I could feel the fear rising in my chest as I tried to explain what had happened. "We were ambushed," I said, my voice squeaky. "We didn't complete the task, but it wasn't our fault. They blindsided us. And you told each of us the other had a pistol."

Jacques scoffed. "Excuses. That's all I ever hear from you two. You were supposed to be prepared for anything. If you can't handle small, aggravated resistance, then you're useless to me." His dismissal felt like a blow to the chest.

Wayne spoke up, his voice shaking. "Inwardly, we overstated our own strength. After what we have seen of our weaknesses being cured, we thought, well...we thought..."

"Spit it out."

I spoke up. "We thought we had the same abilities as you, since you've been feeding us blood."

"We'll do better next time, Jacques. We promise." Wayne put his head in his hands.

It was the first time I had seen my brother truly broken. I felt lost without my pillar of strength in Wayne. We were vulnerable. Jacques's approval was now our very lifeblood and priority. He had given us so much. Asked of us just as much, when you consider murder. Still, we were failures...because we were desperate.

Jacques didn't seem to hear Wayne. "You know what you need?"

he asked, his voice rising. "You need a reminder of yet another house rule. You need to learn that failure is not an option."

My heart sank as I realized what he was saying. He was going to punish us, and it would not be pretty. I looked over at Wayne, and he looked back at me, his eyes wide with fear.

"Come," he ordered.

We obeyed, hoping our submission would count toward our atonement and appreciation of his rule of law.

Jacques led us down to a door, which, to our surprise from what we knew of our city, was a basement.

My heart felt like it was pounding out of my chest. Surely, the strain I continued to put upon it would cause it to explode in due time.

The basement was pitch black.

The stench of wetness and decay hit me as soon as we stepped down the stairs into the enveloping blackness.

I could hear dripping water and the faint moaning of someone in the far reaches of the dungeon-like space.

Jacques struck a match and lit an oil lamp sconce on the wall. "Get in," Jacques said, gesturing to a small room off to the side. "You'll stay here until I decide you've learned your lesson."

Wayne and I hesitated for a moment, then protested and begged that he rethink, but Jacques gave us a shove, and we stumbled into the room.

The door slammed shut behind us, leaving us in complete darkness.

The rancid smell was overwhelming. I tried not to gag. The taste of death was in my mouth, and I knew we were in for a long night. Wayne and I huddled together, trying to find comfort in each other's presence.

From under the door crack, we continued to hear someone moaning. Groaning. Neither Wayne nor I spoke of it. From our limited recall of the parties and strange acts, he and I knew this person was connected. I racked my mind, wondering when I last saw Kesha in the house.

My brother and I sat in silence on the mildewed, filthy ground for what felt like hours. I couldn't tell if it was day or night, and I didn't know how long we would be down there. Uncertain of our fate, my breath became more and more labored.

"I hate him," I concluded.

"You don't. You hate that we can't live up to him. Hate that we are still weak," Wayne corrected me. For the first time, the veil of his unwavering resolve lifted momentarily, and I felt his delusion.

"Wayne, we drank the same blood he appears to drink. How is it we are not yet like him?" I questioned.

"I don't think we've drunk enough. Maybe we need to drink more of his. Eddie said we hadn't turned." Wayne patted my knee in the darkness. "Maybe your true love will come and save us."

I shook away any thought of her, still worried half-to-death that the person groaning in pain might be her. Even if it wasn't, I feared if she attempted our rescue, it would be at great peril to her own safety. "She's a captive here, not unlike us, forced to serve him. She says she has an obligation to the spirits of her ancestors who remain in this house." The intrusive thoughts won, and I couldn't help asking softly, "Wayne, you don't suppose he took our failure out on her, do you? That isn't her we're hearing, is it?"

Wayne expelled a heavy breath of air. "I don't know." His hand squeezed my shoulder. "I think it's best not to know."

"Why won't he just give us the power if he needs us?" I asked.

"Brother, to truly be free, we need to become like Jacques. Become like those who even killed Mother. We have to demand it." The veil lifted once more, and words that should have sounded like perseverance came out more like a fallacy.

"Weren't you listening to Eddie? How can you say such a thing?" I argued. "Become murderers for all eternity, only feeding on the weak?"

I couldn't see Wayne nod, but I knew he had already come to such a resolve. "Then you think he is a true vampire, too."

I had not wanted to say the words to my brother. Saying it to him made it true. The acceptance meant my entire beliefs would be forever changed. My limited knowledge of the world would become much smaller.

Suddenly, the door creaked open, and the silhouette of Jacques stood in the doorway. "You boys ready to return to my world?" he asked, a hint of satisfaction in his voice. "Ready to be redeemed?"

We had no family. Had no money or jobs. Had only escaped poverty through the grace of Jacques. Were we crazy? In hindsight, we would agree, it was sheer fear.

Wayne and I stood and answered without hesitating, "Yes, sir."

Rehabilitation in the relative silence of our tongues and screaming possibilities in our thoughts was complete. Henceforth, we would do as he asked. He was our ticket out of the Hell we had known. We had exchanged it for another Hell, but what options did we have?

Immediately, doubts returned and coursed through my veins. Had we made a mistake in our desperation? It was too late to turn back. Again, the pendulum swung amongst my decisions, trust, and hope.

Jacques led us out of the room and into the main part of the basement. The part from which we could hear the moaning.

Oh, God, not Kesha. Please, not Kesha.

In a corner of the room that was even darker than our own, a form continued the incessant groaning. Rattling chains signaled the person was being kept against their will.

"I'll leave you to it, then," Jacques said as he turned.

"Leave us to what?" I asked, petrified of the answer.

"Make the sniveling and groaning stop," he replied, handing us each two hunting knives. "Return to me when it is finished...and you are full. Consider it a preparation to return to your uncle, where you will complete my request."

Jacques left us in the darkness. It was clear what he expected us to do.

Shoulder to shoulder, I stood with my brother.

I had to know. The words choked from my mouth.

"Kesha?"

CHAPTER 18
SILENCE

What had we become?

I couldn't shake the feeling of utter repulsion and eternal damnation as Wayne and I sloughed through the dimly lit streets of the Swamp on our task. We had failed our job the night before, and the outcome of this second attempt would be our death if it didn't result in the demise of Uncle.

The silence between us was suffocating, and I couldn't bring myself to look at Wayne.

It was he who broke the silence this time. "We're going to finish the job," he said, his voice barely above a whisper. "It doesn't matter how many men."

My heart skipped a beat at his words. "Wayne, they won't be in chains," I replied, my voice trembling. "We couldn't do it last night. How are we going to do it now? I don't feel stronger. Do you?"

"We have to," Wayne said, his eyes blazing with a determination I had never seen before. He didn't even look at me, only ahead. "We can't let Uncle get away with what he did to us. To Father."

I knew he was right, but the thought of killing another person filled me with dread. Doing it in broad daylight made it even worse.

We walked into the rear entrance of Uncle's brothel club, mounting the stairs to his apartment, hoping he would still be asleep while our aunt worked in the bar below. Music and laughter vibrated through the stairs as we climbed, me with mounting trepidation.

The door was in front of us.

We both took deep breaths.

We stepped inside, lying to ourselves that it would be over soon.

Our uncle, as large and intimidating as ever, woke to the sound of our steps, a sneer on his face that turned into full rage at our sight. "What do you want?" he asked, his voice gruff. "Haven't had enough? Will Jacques call and tip me off again to teach you a lesson? I'll kill you boys, right here and now.

"He called you?" We stopped in our tracks.

"Passed word to me to tell the boys. Looks like you bet on the wrong horse. This beating will be straight from me."

"Wait. Just wait." Wayne was processing the unthinkable but couldn't quite pivot through. "We came to talk to you about something else," he said, his voice surprisingly steady. "Something about Mother's death."

Our uncle's face hardened, and I could see the anger in his eyes soften only a hair. "I don't have time for your nonsense," he growled, preparing to leave. "And because you're family and already had your beating, I'll spare you this last time. Know that when you leave, we'll never speak again."

Wayne walked up and grabbed his arm. "Please, Uncle."

I expected a swing from the big man, but it never came.

My brother continued. "We need to know if you've ever heard of vampires in New Orleans. They may have killed her."

Our uncle looked at us like we were crazy. "You boys have lost your minds," he said, rolling up his sleeves, preparing to give us the beating he'd taken off the table. This one would kick us further from his life if we even survived the pummeling.

That's when I pulled out the gun from my waistband.

"Answer him!" I shouted as I raised the weapon.

Wayne looked at me in shock, and I could see the fear in his eyes. We'd come here to do a dark deed, but the one he had prepared would come from his hands. It was always going to be his hands.

"You're mad," Uncle said. "Now put that-"

I aimed the pistol at our uncle's head and pulled the trigger.

The gunshot echoed through the apartment, and I could feel the rush of adrenaline in my head.

The impact blew my uncle against the wall.

A spray of blood flared in splashes, streams, and specks.

Uncle had flopped to the ground, and Wayne was upon him, plunging a knife into his massed belly.

My brother reached into my uncle's chest cavity as if groping blindly for a lost shoe under a sofa. He turned to me with a sinister grin I had not expected in the moment's escalation.

"We should bring Jacques a gift. To celebrate."

I vomited at the sight of the flowing red and mangled flesh, bits of what I'd killed and consumed in the basement spilling all over the floor.

The sight of Wayne's gleeful expression was too much to bear, and I stumbled backward, my body wracked with dry heaves. The thought of our uncle lying there, lifeless, caused me to retch again.

Wayne, on the other hand, seemed unaffected by what had just happened. He wiped the blood off his knife with Uncle's bedding and looked at me with pride and amusement. "We did it, brother," he said. "We got our revenge. For Father. Secured our name."

I couldn't find the words to reply. My mind was reeling, trying to accept what we had just done. The sound of footsteps coming up the stairs snapped me out of my reverie, and I looked around frantically for a place to hide.

Wayne seemed to have the same idea, and we quickly made our way to the balcony, which overlooked the street. We could hear the voices of men approaching, and we knew we had to act fast.

"We have to jump," Wayne said, pointing to the ground below. "It's our only chance."

I looked down at the road below, which seemed impossibly far away. I had never been afraid of heights before, but the prospect of jumping to the ground was something I needed to process.

Wayne must have sensed my hesitation, because he grabbed me by the arm and pulled me toward the balcony's edge. "We have no time," he said. "It's jump or get caught."

With no other options left, I closed my eyes and took a deep breath. And then we jumped.

The fall seemed to last an eternity, and I could feel the wind rushing past me as we plummeted to the ground. I braced myself for my body to crumple, crash and roll. Beside me, I could feel Wayne's body tense.

The impact knocked the wind out of me, and I lay on the ground, gasping for breath. When I finally regained my senses, I looked over at Wayne, who was grinning from ear to ear.

"Come," he said, clapping me on the back. "We're going to make it."

But I knew that wasn't entirely true. The memory of what we had just done would haunt me. Even if we had escaped, there was no telling what would happen next. The men we had heard approaching were likely on our tail, and we did not know where to go or what to do next.

As we stumbled through the alleyways, trying to find a place to hide, I couldn't help wondering if it was all worth it. Had we really avenged our father's death? Or had we just become the men Jacques was creating?

The sound of sirens in the distance brought me back to reality, and I knew we had to keep moving to avoid getting caught. Wayne led the way, scanning the streets for signs of danger.

As we rounded a corner, we came face to face with Eddie. He was frowning at us, his eyes glowing in the shadows of the afternoon shade.

"You've made your choice, I see."

Wayne shook his head. "Our life made our choice for us."

My brother grabbed my hand and pulled me home. To Jacques.

CHAPTER 19
FIGHT

Aside from the run-in with Eddie, one that stayed with me as we ran, Wayne and I escaped under the shadows of our neglected old neighborhood, relieved that anyone else on the street likely had no concern for our presence or was too intoxicated to care. Wayne was bloodied up to his elbows. I carried our prize in a bedroom shoebox. In daylight, we would not pass the scrutiny of the neighborhoods to come. We hid behind an old shed in the coal yard, exchanging glances with one another but not uttering a word.

The dark clouds overhead made it seem like night time was approaching, even though it was only midday. Soon, the clouds burst into showers, and we seized the opportunity to flee and let the heavy rain clean our stains and sins.

Wayne ran beside me, laughing as we splashed the puddles along the way. We felt like kids again, and not the killers we'd become. Blood and burden washed away, we skipped with every step closer to our new home with Jacques. For me, the brutal murder still clung to me, and returning to our mentor with a box containing my uncle's gruesome heart seemed like evidence of a crime I would have preferred to leave behind.

Wayne grinned like a madman. I let the doubts slide to the back of my mind and tried to find some of that joy Wayne seemed to have no issues reveling in.

We made our way inside and up to the second-story library, where Jacques was waiting for us. Kesha, my beautiful Kesha, was also there. I couldn't help feeling a surge of jealousy when I saw the way our host looked at her. She, too, had a most peculiar look that held its own weight.

Jacques appeared pleased when we presented him with the box. "Excellent work, boys," he said, his French accent thick. "Well on your way to regaining my trust. I think you are ready for yet another job, tonight."

"Tonight?" Wayne bristled at the suggestion. "No way. First, we want what you have. We want to be like you. Immortal. Powerful. Uncle told us before he died how you'd set us up for failure the first time."

Jacques let out a cruel laugh. "Failures set up for failure? It's in your nature to fail. You two could never live as blood feasters if you can't even kill right. Until tourism and business return to the Quarter, competition is fierce for survival. Our own business partners can only withstand so much without raising their stakes, to which I would have to oblige. You will do as I say until I decide the time."

For as much as I did not want this life, I found myself trying to reason with him. Perhaps in death, as I currently knew it, my conscience would relax. "But we need to be strong. We need to defend ourselves."

Jacques looked at Kesha, then back at us. "Do you have what it takes?" he asked. "Can you deal with the losses of loved ones? The demise of friends and family. The brutality it takes to not just survive, but thrive?"

I nodded and convinced myself to reply, "Yes." As did my brother.

Wayne added, "We've said as much. How many times have you offered it and taken it back? These are games."

Emboldened by my brother, I straightened my posture and lifted my chin. "You've broken the house rule of trust, Mr. Jacques." His eyes snapped my way.

"Careful. You don't have the stomach, John." His lip snarled. "You're the weakest of the lot and have the most to lose. Show me your dedication. Give me your grit."

"I fired the shot," I boasted, not thinking of how Kesha would respond.

Without warning, Jacques grabbed her by the shoulder and bit down on Kesha's neck. Blood spurted before his lips secured the wound.

Her eyes bulged, and her mouth fell open without a word or scream finding a way out.

Jacques feasted for but a moment. I watched in horror and froze, unable to respond until he tossed her, emotionless, through the terrace doors, and she flopped over the balcony down to the street below.

I took no time before I drew the gun and fired.

Wayne, to my surprise, lunged forward with his knife, stabbing Jacques over and over. The room was filled with our screams of rage and flowed with our host's spilling blood.

When our own massacre of revenge subsided, Wayne and I were, once again, covered in blood and gasping for breath. We looked at each other, and I knew we had crossed a line that could never be undone. We were truly killers now, and I had a feeling this was only the beginning of a new dark and terrifying journey.

Jacques's body remained still in a pool of draining blood. His body was riddled and torn with open gashes and deep mortal wounds. Wayne fell to his knees in tears. He wailed as I rushed to the balcony edge, where I found a small crowd gathered around Kesha, a policeman running her way.

I slumped to my knees, my own legs failing me. She was gone.

"Get away from the balcony, John," Wayne commanded, tempering his volume.

I crawled back to the library. "Wayne, what should we do? If we go outside, the police will surely connect our killing of Jacques to Uncle, but I can't leave Kesha on the street below! I have to help her."

"She's gone, John. They're both gone. Don't you see our predicament?"

"Yes," I agreed. "We'll be tried for our crimes and executed."

"John, no."

"What?" I asked, unsure of what he was referring to.

"Jacques is dead."

"Yes, Wayne, I know. I shot him. Like Uncle. Dead."

"That's just it. He's not supposed to be able to die. I'd shot him before. Didn't I? Wasn't it him? How could he have lived or recovered so quickly before? And now he's just dead?"

I paused at the revelation. "So, what was he?"

Head in his hands, Wayne wailed, "Nothing! He was nothing, John!"

"We killed an innocent man?"

"He wasn't innocent, John. He had us kill for him. He...used us."

"But Wayne, for what purpose? What could he have wanted from us? From Uncle?"

A revelation hit Wayne. "Business. Simple business. Power. And favors. Jacques said it himself. Uncle wanted to expand. To bring the red light clubs to this area down from Storyville. But his high society friends wouldn't want that. So, while Uncle's men were killing grocers and the Italians started moving to the other districts, Jacques and his friends were likely taking advantage of this. *You* retrieved the axe."

"How does that benefit others to the cost of ourselves?"

"I don't know. Maybe it helped them buy properties. Opening new businesses?"

I slid my legs out from under me and sat with my brother. "So the lying bastard was nothing but a vampire wannabe piece of crap. And who was in the basement?"

He shrugged. "I haven't seen Terrance, have you?"

The thought was beyond comprehension. "Oh, my dear, Kesha. Why didn't we leave when we could?"

Wayne stared at Jacques in complete disbelief. He crawled over to our dead host and lifted his lips. "He bit her with just regular teeth. Long maybe, but regular teeth."

"What if it takes time? Maybe he'll heal over time like we did." I almost couldn't believe Jacques was just a man.

Wayne stood and exited the room, returning with the trombone case. "Wayne?"

He opened the instrument and retrieved the axe, which he hefted and snapped down on Jacques's neck. The head rolled to the side, eyes open but lifeless.

Wayne huffed a heavy sigh. "Well, let's see how that grows back."

There were knocks on the door downstairs, but we dared not answer, knowing it was the authorities.

Wayne and I cleaned ourselves and changed clothes, then pilfered and plundered all the monies, gold coins, and valuables we could carry. It was time for our second escape of the day.

I guided Wayne through the narrow corridors and cut-throughs.

"John, where are you taking us?"

"I may know someone who can help."

"John, no one can know!"

If this person is real, she already knows.

CHAPTER 20
FALLOUT

We left from the back courtyard, and in a short time he and I had weaved a circuitous route and found ourselves at last at the door of Mama Loca.

The door was locked.

I hammered on the wood, to no avail.

"John, what are we doing here?"

"Kesha's aunt. She's a-"

The door opened. Mama Loca said nothing. She turned and walked back inside her home.

"Mama Loca," I said. "We -"

"You've brought to my home only death."

Wayne looked at me, confused.

"I'm so sorry, Mama Loca. I'm afraid your niece-"

"Is gone," she interjected.

"Yes," I whispered.

"She wanted to give you a gift. She tried to protect you."

"It was Jacques," I shared, knowing she would well know who. "I wasn't strong enough to stop him. We were afraid of what he would do to us; what we thought he could do to us." My head hung low. "He was just a man."

She waved her finger in the air. "Not all vampires walk with the dead."

Wayne shook his head. "He's dead. He didn't get back up. He's not coming back."

Mama Loca shot her finger again. "Not undead. He was human. He was evil. He was compelled, as were you. He believed in himself more than you didn't believe in him. He drew power. Energy. Fed from it. He still may change. The danger is not over."

"I won't fear a Jacques walking around with no head."

"Take the head off a snake; it can still kill you. Take the head of a two-headed snake; it can still find you. You must leave," she warned. "But first, I have something for you."

She produced a small jar and two cups from a top shelf. She poured a thick, dark liquid for them both. "Drink."

We both declined.

"We're done." I pushed the cups back.

She pushed them forward. "Your danger has just begun. You came for help. Drink. It's what Kesha would want. If you do not want, then go."

Wayne stepped away. "Voodoo. Vampires. It was snake oil. Fraud."

Mama Loca stood and went to the cupboard. "Does your leg work?"

"Yes," Wayne replied. "It was probably a coincidence. Something else. Let's go, John." He made for the door. I grabbed ahold of his shirt and pulled him back. It was my turn to know better, and his turn to be confused and go along with things.

Within Mama Loca's hand was a small figurine of cloth and stick. It looked to be a plaything of a child who could not afford a doll. She twisted the figure's leg, and my brother fell to the floor with a wail of excruciating pain. She twisted the other leg of the straw doll.

Wayne fell backward, writhing in agony.

I jumped to my feet. "Stop! You're killing him."

"Mama is teaching." She pushed the doll's arms up with her thumbs, and my brother rose to his.

She then smoothed the legs, waved a hand over the object, and my brother fell silent, all pain removed.

"Come," she said to me and my brother. "Drink the magic if you wish to live."

The drink was like the blood we'd had before in smell and texture. This, however, burned. It was liquid fire, and the drink scorched our insides and drew tears from our eyes.

After we wiped our lids dry, Mama Loca was nowhere to be found.

Wayne and I gathered our belongings, not sure what to do next.

Fate was hawking outside the door.

As we exited the hidden storefront, New Orleans police were waiting to question us.

The police dragged me and my brother Wayne into the parish station. We had been spotted fleeing a crime scene as we ran through the French Quarter, and upon taking us into custody, they had found us with all of Jacques's valuables - his money, jewels, everything.

As they questioned us, I could tell they didn't believe our story. We told them we hadn't seen Jacques in days. They said a woman had claimed Jacques had attacked her and thrown her from his balcony.

Kesha.

"She's alive?" I blurted.

"You know the woman?" The officer leaned in closer.

"I know she was...um, a house girl."

He squinted. "Did they get along? Was he abusive toward her? Colored girl?"

I shrugged. "French, I think. I'm sure Jacques could tell you better than I."

"Where did you say you were from again, Mr. Carter? You sound like an educated man, but you don't quite fit the behavior."

Wayne interjected, "We're gentlemen. And we agree such behavior would be beneath us."

I side-eyed my brother as he bit his lip to keep from grinning.

The officers would have to fight for any sort of confession. With the news of Kesha being alive and both a foreigner and free person of color, this would not be a priority case.

Wayne and I were in deep trouble, but perhaps not just yet.

My confidence became emboldened. "Did you ask the houseman, Terrance?" I'm sure he could provide the information you seek.

The officer leaned in close to us. "Jacques St. Germain's house," he consulted his notes, "at ten thirty-nine Royal Street, is completely empty. No furniture, no wall hangings, no curtains, no rugs. All of it was empty, save for corked bottles of wine that didn't have wine in them. Do you know what they were filled with?"

My brother and I both shrugged, knowing the contents. I, curious about the missing axe.

"I'll ask again. Where is he?" the officer snapped.

Wayne piped up one more time. "What about the basement?" he asked. "Did you check there?"

"Funny. There are no basements in the Quarter."

With that remark, Wayne and I looked at one another, confused.

The police had nothing on us aside from the riches, but with no one claiming they were missing, this was also not an immediate threat. Still, they pressed again, wanting to know where we had gotten all the valuables from, but before I could answer, a figure walked in the door.

Eddie the Glove.

"You can't be in here, Detective," the policeman said. "Sorry, ex-Detective."

Eddie nodded in understanding. "Just wanted to give you my two bits. The boys are late for a delivery to a couple of my clients. They never made it after making a drop of herbs to Mama Loca."

"These guys work for you?"

Eddie nodded again. "Couriers from time to time. Today, they're not on time." Eddie checked his watch.

"They stay with Jacques St. Germain. He's wanted for biting a woman and tossing her off the balcony."

"The boys have been staying with me until they find a place of their own. My neighbors can vouch for them. You just need to be willing to step into the Tremé and ask around."

The officers side-eyed one another. The Tremé was a historic African-American community just north of the Quarter where free persons of color and prior African slaves could acquire and own property. A place these men rarely frequented.

The officers seemed skeptical, but they let us go for the time being. The riches we'd liberated from Jacques, however, stayed in police protection.

We were back to where we started when we'd first met Him.

As we walked out of the station, I felt relief mixed with fear. We had narrowly escaped being caught, but I knew this wouldn't be the end.

Jacques was gone; for how long, we didn't know, but we had heard of the Others. Whether it was a fable like Jacques, I felt revenge in one form or another was closing in on us.

Our minds were whirling.

"Thanks for your help, Eddie." Wayne extended a hand. If it was one thing Jacques had taught us, it was some of the little things of becoming a gentleman. Still, I was desperate for news of Kesha's condition.

"Eddie, have you heard anything about Kesha?" I asked, my voice shaking with emotion.

He shook his head. "I have heard nothing yet, but I'll check with the hospital. If she spoke to the police, that's a good sign. Are you boys sure you don't know where he is?"

Wayne and I exchanged nervous glances. We didn't want to reveal too much, but we also knew we needed Eddie's help.

"We don't know exactly where he is," Wayne said carefully. "But we believe he's still in the city."

Eddie seemed suspicious of us, but he didn't press any further. Instead, he asked us where we were going to live.

"We don't know," I said, feeling a sense of desperation creeping up on me. I hadn't thought that far ahead.

Eddie looked at us closely in the bright sun. The light hurt our eyes, but there were no signs of redness or blistering on our skin. Clearly a myth anyway, packaged with the lies Jacques fed us.

"I know of a place on the corner of Royal and St. Anne," he said. "I can get you jobs on the docks, working for the shipyard and fishing boat. It's not glamorous, but it'll keep you fed. An honest day's work for an honest day's pay."

I felt a glimmer of hope at his words. Maybe there was a chance for us after all. Maybe we could put this nightmare behind us. As we followed Eddie down the street, I wondered what other dangers lay ahead of us in this city and if we would ever truly be safe again. After our experience with Jacques, could we even trust Eddie?

CHAPTER 21
FATIGUE

We sat in the disregarded chairs we'd found on the streets. We were loomed by the old mattress we had carried to our apartment on the second floor. The room was dimly illuminated by one flickering light bulb and filled with the musty smell of decay. In these strange surroundings, we were hungry and restless. We couldn't sleep.

As I looked around the old and neglected room, I felt a pang of longing for our life with Jacques. Life was horrible with such a beast, but luxurious and in some perverse way—safe. We had everything, although nothing was our own. Be it a dream or a nightmare, those days were gone, and we had to survive by what we could scavenge.

Wayne broke the silence. "John, our weakness may be because of a lack of blood. We need more blood. We could be stronger if we drank more. Be more like Jacques."

I could not imagine killing anyone else. I wanted that life behind me. "I don't know, Wayne. I don't even know what to think or do. What's the point? It was one thing to have Jacques around, filling our heads with promise, but why do it? It's easier to steal day-old bread."

"You heard it from the old lady. You can hear. I can walk better.

You are no longer fainting. Something worked. Every time we drink, we feel better, but it doesn't last. We need to drink as often as we would eat. Maybe instead of eating. I only saw Jacques consume from a cup." Wayne leaned forward, with intense eyes. "What if we discovered people who were doing bad things? What if we only fed on those who were bad people, vagabonds, or drunken sailors from far-off places? Then we could use some of their blood to set them free. No one would miss them."

As the memory of Kesha falling from the balcony washed over me, I felt despair. With Jacques's money and hospitality gone, how long would my brother's healed leg last? How long before I started fainting again? Jacques wasn't around to shower us with gifts anymore, but I'd be damned if I'd let this gift slip through my fingers.

"Fine. Fine. We'll do it your way, but only if you can find someone deserving. We must let them go."

He vowed, "We will let them go."

The decision was made. We were hanging on to legend. Fantasy. Heading to delusion and ultimate madness. I, holding on to hope. My brother, fighting his immeasurable fear of death.

We wandered the streets that night, in search of our next victim. As we searched for a target who met Wayne's requirements, the darkness seemed to swallow up our search. As we snuck through the narrow alleyways, my heart beat fast.

My mind was racing as we finally found the right person.

I was immediately on board.

A drunk man was beating a woman just a few blocks away from

The Swamp. She was most likely a prostitute, but an undeserving victim nonetheless. We would do her a favor. Do the city a good deed.

Wayne, with a brick in hand, snuck behind the man.

He delivered a swift blow to the drunk's head, who fell to his knees but was not down for good.

The man tried to thwart Wayne's next attack, flashing a blade through the air that almost caught my brother's stomach.

I had a backup knife and pounced. I sank it as deep as possible into his stomach, twisting until the man stopped his struggle.

The woman fled, screaming.

We tried to lift the man, but he was either too heavy or we were too weak.

"John, we won't make it back. Let's do it right here."

My brother lifted the shirt of the fresh corpse and drank the blood from the wound.

He then turned and bid my participation.

I slurped the fountain of life flowing from our victim. As I drank, a strange surge of power swept through me. For a moment, it was as if I had found what we sought and all my doubts were washed down with the blood.

We were careful not to question what we'd done as we cleaned up. Promises of strength and eternal life? The promise was still not fulfilled short of renewed strength, which was enough for the day. It was something, and our bellies were full again.

Wayne appeared to be wrestling with the same issues as I was. He tried to hide it behind his bravado. He made jokes about our newfound freedom, and how we could do anything we wanted without fearing the wrath of Jacques or his consequences. His eyes revealed his inner turmoil, and I knew he was as lost as me.

We tried to adapt to our new reality. We became stronger, and we mastered our capture and attack.

Each night, we explored the city, taking from the unknowing and unaware. We felt powerful, invincible. We felt less guilty for our actions, and with our own memories enabled, we cast away the thoughts of the dark deeds we committed. We'd grown rabid and mad.

As we walked through the city streets, we came across a group of laughing and joking young men. We could smell their alcohol from across the street. They were carefree and drunk. Wayne's eyes gleamed, and I could tell what was on his mind. A test of our improved skills.

He had already crossed the street before I followed. The group laughed at him and teased him, unaware of the danger. Wayne flashed the blade, and I knew it was too late for me to join in the first wave of attack.

I watched him feed on them, hearing their screams in my ears. My brother had become something of himself, indeed. Who needed to be a vampire when we had the power to be rippers?

As the nights wore on, our promises of ridding the streets of evil were soon forgotten. We started taking anyone we could. Innocent or otherwise. We had an entire apartment of feeders in no time. Some of them we bled, others we fed. Our addiction grew beyond control.

Life from before seemed to slip from our consciousness, replaced with a hunger and need we could never fill for long. It was as if our minds had tapped into something primal. Nothing else mattered, but we were still not as strong as Jacques. We couldn't convince anyone to join us. We had to use force but were never beaten back. The power was intoxicating. It was only after we'd fed on that young girl, freed her, and left for the docks that humanity slapped me in the face with the morning sun. A sad life of debauchery and crime crashed back into my conscience, and I turned and begged Wayne that we stop. We'd gone too far and lost ourselves once more, and this time Jacques wasn't to blame. No green fairies, no imposing master. Just us and all the blood I could never wash from my hands or my soul. I wanted to see it end, even if that meant the end of life itself. We had abandoned our own charter. We had lost. We had lost it all.

Wayne watched my meltdown with little care but said something that would change our destiny.

"If that is what you want, let her leave. I'm tired, John."

CHAPTER 22
JUDGMENT

Her name, Alyson Adnarok. We saw her on the missing notices pasted about the Quarter.

She was much younger than we thought when we took her. I'm not sure we even cared.

When I released her, it hadn't taken long for the police to find our living quarters. They found our other victims still bound and those we had left dead in another room as we contemplated whether their meat might sustain us and our captives.

They found us, too, but Wayne and I were able to fight them off and flee.

"Where can we go, Wayne?" I remember asking as we hid among the shipping containers and vessels docked at the port.

"I thought we could do it, brother. I thought we would make a name for ourselves." He cried uncontrollably, and I could not find any words of comfort. Whatever was coming for us...we deserved it.

When we were discovered again, we did not resist.

This time, they took us straight to the Old Parish Prison, home of the infamous Sicilian Lynchings. A dark and dangerous home of the convicted and condemned where corrupt guards would stand aside to mob murder within their high stone walls and iron gates. A place I'd spied before, as I contemplated our fate.

Music stopped that day, for the third time, as word of our horrors spread through the Quarter.

The trial went quickly, as did our conviction and sentence. Eddie was there, warning the judge to commit us to a sanitarium and spare New Orleans from our death.

The judge ruled against us...and Eddie. Better times were coming again for New Orleans, and the reputation of the city nearing the end of Prohibition was not to be sullied, so there was a brief mention of our preying on the people of the Quarter. They wanted us gone.

Days before our hanging, I had accepted that Wayne and I deserved our punishment for what we had done and were likely driven to do again. And yet, I couldn't shake the hunger that gnawed at my insides, craving the taste and smell of life on my tongue. As we sat in our cell, waiting for our inevitable execution, a sense of shuddersome settled over me. I thought of Kesha and whether she knew what had happened to me or very much cared. Oh, the life we could have had together. We could have been happy. During the trial, Eddie never passed word to us on her condition or whereabouts, and when we did finally receive a message, it was because he had made arrangements to have us buried in our family vault. Under our family name. That no one would find the Carter Brother vampires.

The Carter Brothers would be no more.

It was then the police came into our cell at night. They said nothing, but I knew what was coming. I was to be hung first. Then Wayne. The thought of being executed filled me with fear, but also a strange liberation. At least it would be over. Our insignificant lives would be wiped from the world with no memory of us, save for our evil deeds, which would also fade in time. Someone would have finally stopped us, because we were never going to stop ourselves.

"We're together, John," my brother said. "Forever. We tried to find a family but had each other the whole time. I failed you."

And in that moment, I knew even death couldn't separate us. We would be trapped in that vault together for eternity as our flesh fell from bone. The thought was unsettling but also comforting. No one understood our peril but us, and we would suffer together.

They placed the rope around my neck and gave it a tight tug. I thought of our victims' wrists as we were given the last cinch and a good pull.

A black hood was placed over my head.

There was about a minute of silence. I listened for the voice of my brother. I recalled the voice of my dear Kesha, and the warnings of Eddie we'd failed to heed.

As the floor under my feet fell, and the weight of my body followed, I recalled the laugh of Jacques in my mind, saying, "They were troubled boys. Troubled indeed."

The rope offered our short lives no more of its length and came to a snapping halt.

I saw the green fairy again. She smiled, and spread her lips wide, displaying rows of sharp jagged teeth until the images of my mind darkened and were covered with the black hood of death.

It was done.

CHAPTER 23
NIGHTMARE

I awake to excruciating, eye-watering pain, writhing in torture. It feels as though my body is being ripped apart without end, even when I think there is nothing more to shred. But then, as quickly as the pain comes, it subsides. I feel a change happening within me, and an incredible hunger and rage emerge. My body convulses as my organs reanimate, one by one. My chest is tight, and my head is screaming in agony.

I open my eyes but can't see anything.

It's pitch dark. As if the world outside has ceased to exist and I am trapped in a nightmare. My arms and legs stuck. Confined.

There's heat around me like a furnace, and I feel my face blistering and burning. I get a sudden shock, as I realize I am not alone.

I feel a body pressing against mine. We're tight.

The sweat drips from my forehead and face, leaving warm, wet trails on the back of my neck and head.

My chest tightens painfully, and I frantically gasp for air.

It feels like walls are closing around me and there's no way to escape. How long will I be trapped here? My mind falls down a never-ending spiral of being stuck forever. Minutes turn to hours, or have they been mere seconds? I don't dare to see who is pressed against me, but my muscles cramp, and my body aches...I can't stay like this much longer.

My voice is hoarse, but I whisper, "Wayne." As the words pass, they sting my throat. I use my elbow, which has no leverage, to nudge him.

My brother remains still and silent, adding to my fear. I don't know if he's alive or dead. Suddenly, it feels like reality is frozen for a moment. Time feels off. It dawns on me that I'm probably constantly passing out from lack of oxygen, though the awareness doesn't stop it from happening. It's my nightmare come to life. I'm trapped in a loop, with no way out. Each time I wake up, I pray, trying to find some solace in any faith known to man. The only thing that keeps me going is the thought that this is some mistake. That someone will figure it out and come find us. This isn't my forever.

I try to move my feet and extend them against the hard buttress. It moves. They move. Bones. There are bones at the base of our feet.

We're buried alive, sealed in this tomb.

Wayne groans beside me, and I can feel his panic rising.

"Wayne. It's me. It's okay. Breathe."

"I can't. I can't breathe. Where are we? What's happened?"

He begins his own struggle of desperation for a long while, trying to find a way out. As his fear builds, I'm pressed tighter and tighter into the walls. My face pushed to the hot entombment. We've taken all the air, passing out and coming to in an endless cycle. The fear in my heart is too much to bear. I pray for death and feel my body shaking uncontrollably.

We're fighting each other for space, soaked in our sweat. Baking in the scorching Louisiana summer heat, undead and ever dying a horror no doubt as a curse for our deeds.

We hear something hitting the brick and mortar behind our heads, and we both stop our struggle. It's getting louder and louder. One by one, the bricks crumble, and we're hit with a blast of warm air. It cools as our sweat evaporates from our skin.

Before I can even relish in my freedom, I smell the scent of human blood in the air, and immediately it becomes all I can think about. My instincts take over, and I know I must satisfy my thirst. Something dark and primal. So much different than before.

Hands grab us, and we're yanked out of complete darkness to the cloud-covered light of the moon.

We both gasp for air, and I look up to see Terrance, the house-man, standing before us.

"Terrance. My God. What's happening?" I ask, still struggling to speak properly.

Terrance doesn't answer me. Instead, he points to a woman standing beside him. She's unfamiliar, and I can't quite make out her features in the night. A disturbing wave washes over me, and I realize something is terribly wrong.

Behind Terrance and the unfamiliar woman stands Mama Loca and my beloved Kesha. At her side is a man, the likeness of an old painting I saw in the home of Jacques, one he referred to as a relative, the Count de St. Germain.

Wait. Haven't I seen him before? The two Jacques. Was it he we first met?

The sight of them sends a chill down my spine, and I can feel Wayne shaking beside me as he tries to control his own mounting hunger.

Kesha offers me no greeting. No look of love lost. She steps forward past the witch, her eyes fixed on the unfamiliar woman. "Take her," she orders, her voice low and menacing. "And feed." She turns and takes the hand of the count before walking away, with Mama Loca trailing close behind.

"Wait! Kesha."

Terrance presses his finger to my lips and grabs my arm. "She said, feed."

I do.

At that first bite, as the blood leaves its beautiful host and courses through my awakened veins, the stolen memories unfold and flood my mind. Clarity surrounds me. We'd been bewitched by the vampire herself, compelled to act and forget. Perhaps even Jacques, a mortal in the end, had fallen to the vampire's spell, whether my love's or his own ancestry. Still, there were abilities he had I still can't rationalize. Secrets perhaps I will learn in this new life of the living dead.

As my brother feeds next to me, I watch as Kesha and her small enclave walk toward the Lafayette Cemetery exit.

Would we follow?

As I stand outside our family's tomb, I can feel the wind blowing against every fiber of my hair, kissing the gooseflesh on my arm, the rustling of each leaf on the bordering trees, and the sound of every cricket for miles. It's as if my senses are heightened beyond what a human can fathom and I am completely immersed, at one with my surroundings. The clouds overhead part, revealing a full and bright moon that casts a soft glow over everything. In the distance, I can hear the haunting howls of a wolf from the bayou, its mournful cry echoing through the night. And then, faintly, I hear the distant sound of jazz music coming from the Quarter, its notes carrying on the wind.

THE END

ABOUT THE AUTHOR

J.T. Patten is an emerging author of horror stories. This is J.T.'s sixth dark fiction book. He is an active member of the Horror Writers Association and International Thriller Writers. His initial best-selling works have gained acclaim for their "blacker than black" brooding narrative that illuminate the blurred lines in life and twist traditional tropes on their head.

He has a degree in Foreign Language, a Masters in Strategic Intelligence, graduate studies in Counter Terrorism from the University of St. Andrews.

More information about JT and his works can be found at www.jtpattenbooks.com

Also by J.T. Patten

Horror

Whispers of a Gypsy

Thrillers

Shadow Masters

Primed Charge

Presidential Retreat

Buried in Black

Presence of Evil

www.ingramcontent.com/pod-product-compliance
Lightning Source LLC
Chambersburg PA
CBHW022029170626
46808CB00003B/1117